FELIX FEATHERSTONE and The Way of The Wolveraffes

FELIX FEATHERSTONE and The Way of The Wolveraffes

The Hollow Island Trilogy (Part 1)

Daniel Turnpike

HERBRAND PRESS

Contents

PUBLISHED BY HERBRAND PRESS 2024

HERBRAND PRESS,
BERNARD MANSIONS,
HERBRAND STREET
LONDON WC1N 1LB

First Published, 2024
ISBN 978-1-3999-7083-9

ILLUSTRATIONS by ROBERT STOCKS

{ 1 }

Secrets and Lies

Felix loved silence. Especially in the classroom. It's the only time that he could hear himself think. It's the only time that he could see things clearly in his mind.

He could never understand how he was supposed to work out the values of x and y when Daryll was accusing him of stealing his rubber, Talisha was telling him about her cat hitting his head against the window last night and Tyrone was tapping his pencil and singing some rap song about how much he hated maths. That was three things too many going on in his head when all he wanted was one!

But the morning of November 29th wasn't like that. That morning, there was silence, and it was far too precious, far too peaceful for anyone to want to break. Daryll had found his rubber, Talisha was daydreaming about her cat, and Felix was on the verge of cracking the 'x + y equals z' problem that Jermaine had set him. Even Tyrone seemed to be happy, curled up round his desk, getting on with his sums and wallowing in the warmth and tranquillity of it all.

This silence really could have been golden, had Felix not suddenly realised that he'd made a mistake in his working out which made all the rest of his calculations wrong – so completely and utterly wrong that he picked up his exercise book and threw it as hard as he could onto the floor.

'Felix!' said Ms Bird, looking down at the book, which was splayed out over the carpet. 'Do you want to...um?'

Felix's deep blue eyes were staring intensely at his desk and his skinny little arms, poking out through the frayed cuffs of his blazer, were wrapped around the top of his head. He wasn't going to answer. But after a couple of deep breaths, he thought better of it.

'No, it's all right, miss. I think I'm OK now.'

'Good. Well, in that case,' said Ms Bird, 'we'll move on to Geometry. Monitors!'

The noise level jumped from one to a hundred within seconds and order turned into disorder. Felix was still too annoyed with himself to join in though. So, he opened up his assessment book, only to find a crumpled-up piece of paper, smelling of stale lemon juice, with a handwritten message on it:

> *Please take this note when no one is looking, particularly your teacher, and put it into your pocket. You may read it at your leisure when you are in a private place, but you will have to hold it up to a light bulb first, as what follows is written in invisible ink.*

Felix folded it in half, slipped it into his back pocket while Ms Bird was busy changing the slides on the interactive whiteboard, and put his hand up just as she turned round to talk to the class.

'Felix, it's my turn now. You can ask your questions afterwards.'

'Sorry, miss, but I...'

'You need to go out?'

'Yes.'

'So, you **are** having...'

'...Yes.'

'You do pick your moments, don't you? This means that you'll have missed all the instructions. All right. I can see...'

'Thank you, miss,' he said as he headed for the door.

You should probably know that Felix was one of those kids who got angry very easily and had to leave the classroom a lot. But wouldn't you if you kept getting the blame for just about everything that went wrong at home? The stupid thing was that *home* was the only place where he didn't have any outbursts. That's probably because if he did, his dad would have had an even bigger one. And you didn't want to be around when that was happening.

Although he was only supposed to go into the corridor for his cool-downs, he needed somewhere much more private for this. So, he made a beeline for the toilets and held the note up to one of the light bulbs in there. As soon as the invisible ink had come through, he went straight into a cubicle, put the seat down, perched himself on top of it and started reading:

Hello. I have been asked to contact you as you have been selected to take part in a special activity, which I can't, for reasons of security, tell you any more about at the moment. What I can do though is to ask you a question: Have you ever wondered what it must be like to do things which change people's lives? Or even to become a bit of a hero? If you have, what I'm going to tell you about might well interest you. If you would like to hear more, please tear off the smiley emoji at the bottom of this piece of paper and stick it onto the face of your watch. If you're not interested, please put the sad face emoji there instead. Whatever your decision, please tear this note up as soon as you have read it.

They had been given so many warnings about not talking to strangers or answering messages online, but this was not

online. This was at school. So, he could probably trust that part of it and then see what happened next. He thought that he might as well follow this up and at least see if it was genuine. If he was asked to do anything which felt suspicious, he could put a stop to the whole thing and report it. For the moment however, he would keep this all to himself.

And that's when it all started. Or at least that's when Felix thought it had all started. There was something else before that though – only he didn't realise it at the time. This new girl in his class, Edith – the one with rosy cheeks and pigtails, who wanted to save the planet – had come up to him, wanting to know if she could have a look at his Ghostbuster socks. Although they weren't particularly spectacular, she seemed to be dead impressed and asked him if he was going to the Halloween party at school that year. He said that there was nothing he liked more than dressing up as the devil and scaring people, but it never worked in the school hall, especially since the teachers insisted on keeping all the lights on. She thought that sounded really crumby and said that if he liked proper Halloween, then he would love the party she was going to. When he asked her what that was, she said that she couldn't tell him, that it was a secret, that it was far too cool for school, but that he would definitely find out about it sometime.

And now there was this. A message in his exercise book. Had he ever dreamed of changing people's lives or even becoming a bit of a hero? Yes, most of his life if he was honest. Scoring a goal in the World Cup Final, doing a ten-minute guitar solo on stage at Wembley or abseiling down the Empire State Building. You bet he'd dreamed of being a hero. The answer had to be 'YES'. On the way back to the classroom, he licked the back of the smiley emoji and stuck it onto his Fitbit. It looked a bit odd, but no one seemed to notice although **someone** must have done because later in the morning, he found another note – in his Science book this time.

As it had the same instruction as last time about holding it up to a light, he folded it in half and put it into his blazer pocket.

'Anything interesting, Felix?' said Mr King.

'No, sir. It's nothing.'

'Well then you won't mind if I have a look at it. You know what the rules are. Bring it up.'

Felix just sat there speechless, rubbing his hand up and down his leg. Luckily, Jermaine – who had been using his fuzzy mop of hair to conceal the fact that he was drawing – lifted his head and put his hand up.

'Yes, Jermaine.'

'Excuse me, sir. That was my fault. I passed that note to Felix. It's just one of my sketches,' he said, pretending to take Felix's note from him, but then holding up a similar looking piece of paper in the air.

'Well, bring it up then.'

So, Jermaine took his drawing up to the teacher's desk and Mr King examined it.

'And who's this supposed to be?'

'You, sir.'

There were titters all around the classroom.

'Perhaps this won't be quite so funny after you've missed all your breaktimes for the rest of the week.'

'No, sir. It won't, sir.'

So, Jermaine had saved his bacon. And this was not the first time. In fact, ever since primary school, when Felix threw the class football over the fence at break time, he'd been his saviour. Jermaine would always stick up for a friend in need and not worry about the consequences. He was far too cool to have to go along with the crowd. You only had to take one look at him to see that. If it wasn't for him, Felix's life at school would have been hell. At lunchtime, he wanted to thank him for what he'd done but he didn't get the chance because, of course, he was in detention. So, he had to wait until the end of school and after Jermaine had finished at Taekwondo.

'That note better've had some **serious** stuff in it,' said Jermaine.

'I think it is kind of serious,' said Felix as they walked out of the gates and headed off down the road. 'I haven't read it yet though.'

'What d'ya mean – you haven't... You've only had all lunchtime.'

'I know, but you can't find anywhere private at lunch-time. It's written in invisible ink, so I need to...'

'Oh, well. Now you're talking. The King would've loved to have got his claws on that.'

'Why did he get so vexed about your picture of him, by the way? I mean, you usually get people exactly right.'

'Because it wasn't him. But I had to make it sound like

it was. Otherwise, why would you be looking like you've just taken twenty quid out of your dad's wallet?'

'Oh. I see. Who was it then?' said Felix, as Jermaine opened his front door and let himself in.

'Dracula!' he called back.

'Legend, Jermaine. You're a legend,' shouted Felix as he raced off down the road and into The Under.

Now, in case you don't know what The Under is, I should tell you that Felix lives on the fifteenth floor of a block of flats. Directly below his bedroom window is a vast network of flyovers. And underneath this unruly jumble of concrete is The Under. They call it The Under because it's underlit, underpopulated, under-inhabited, underdeveloped and under the motorway, of course. All in all, it's under everything and it's a place that Felix spent quite a lot of time in. It's not school and it's not home. It's just The Under. Whoever he wanted to be he could be down there. But not today. Today, he needed to get back to the flat.

As soon as the lift arrived at the fifteenth floor of Trevelyan Tower, Felix made a dash for his front door and steadied his shaking hand as he tried to get the key in the lock. Once inside, he called out to check that no one was home.

'Dad!'

'About time too. Just doing you a fry up,' his dad shouted from the kitchen.

'Oh, OK,' said Felix, heading for the sitting room, where he turned on the dimmer switch, stood on a chair and held the note up to a dangling lightbulb.

'Felix!'

'Yes, Dad.'

'Come on! Your tea will be ruined.'

'Coming.'

'What you doing in the...?'

'Oh, I just need to do something.'

'Come and have your tea first.'

'OK,' he said as the words were beginning to appear. Something about going to a special island.

'I said...'

'Yes, Dad.'

Felix crumpled up the note, put it into his pocket and went into the disaster area that was their kitchen.

'Well, you can't say I don't try and look after you. Here you are,' said his dad, as he laid down a plate in front of him with dried up bacon, rubberised egg, that you could throw against the wall and catch, and shrivelled mushrooms, just like his great grandma's fingers used to look.

'Serves you right. Taste of your own medicine,' said his dad.

'What do you mean?'

'Well...everything **you** touch turns to ashes. This is all because you didn't come when I called you,' he said, looking at the grease on his hand and wiping it on his jeans. 'What were you doing in the living room?'

'Just doing something for my homework.'

'What?'

'Oh, nothing important.'

'So, nothing important takes priority over my fry up, does it? You know, sometimes I think you're doing this deliberately. Because there's only one of me...Anyway, sit down and eat your tea.'

'I'm not being rude, but that egg will make me throw up.'

'Well...Just make sure you do that in the toilet then.'

'My teeth aren't strong enough for...'

'For what?'

'Nothing, Dad.'

Bits of rubbery egg were sticking to the side of his teeth and the hard, sharp shards of bacon cut into his gums and the side of his mouth.

'You better not be late for your tea tomorrow,' said his dad. 'Lauren's coming round to do you a birthday dinner.'

'Ah, OK.'

'Well, don't sound so enthusiastic.'

'Oh, sorry. Yeah, great.'

'You'll probably be seeing quite a bit more of her from now on.'

'Oh, OK.'

As his dad turned to look out of the window, Felix pulled a plastic bag – from Science – out of his pocket, shoved as much food into it as he could and put it onto his lap.

'Can't believe that tomorrow will be eleven years since your mum passed away,' said his dad as he stroked his sideburns.

'No.'

'Well, despite all your complaints, you've gobbled that lot up.'

'Yes, Dad. I better go and finish my homework now.'

'Right. Well, I'm off to the pub for a swift one.'

'Do you want me to stack the dishwasher?'

'No, mate. Not unless you've got the odd three hundred quid to spare,' he said. 'Bad enough you breaking everything in your room, let alone in the kitchen. These appliances cost a lot of money, you know. Anyways, I'll be back in two shakes.'

'OK,' said Felix, wondering whether he might at least be able to do a sneaky wash of some of his stinky shirts while his dad was out. The ones that his dad was supposed to have done last week. But no. There were far more important things to do. He went straight to his room and pulled out the note:

Hello, again. Thanks for putting the smiley emoji on your watch. Now I can tell you what this is all about. You may not be aware of it but there is a day in our calendar called Holloween. It's a bit like Halloween, only it's on the last day of November instead of the last day in October. Anyway, it's kind of the opposite of Halloween, but also very similar, if you get me. On Halloween, the wall between the Earth and another dimension thins and all the spirits and ghosts come through just for that night and then return from whence they came as if nothing had happened. On Holloween, it's the other way round. It's us that go through the wall, not to where the ghosts are but to a special island on planet Tritan. A place where you will flourish and discover your hidden – maybe even heroic – depths. I went last year, and I wouldn't have missed it for... well... anything. By the way, you get brought back here before daylight on December 1st. If you are *interested in joining us, please post your reply on the pillar next to the maintenance shed in The Under. But no names, please. 'FF wants to go,' will do the job just fine.*

A chance to discover his heroic depths! For the boy who turns everything into ashes! The boy who's terrified of doing anything in case it causes a catastrophe! Maybe this was his opportunity to prove himself once and for all.

There wasn't any time to lose. He quickly fished out a bit of paper, some double-sided tape and a sharpie from the table drawers and hurriedly wrote the note. As soon as he'd stuck some tape on the back of it, he went out of the front door, headed down to The Under, chucked his plastic bag full of food into a bin and stuck the note on the pillar.

It was only after he'd got back to the flat and made himself comfortable on his bed that he wondered what he'd just signed himself up to? What were they going to make him do there? What if he made a mess of things – like he always did – and ended up in disgrace with nowhere to hide. At least in this world he could come back to his own room. And play his games on the computer. And be a superhero without anyone getting in his way.

Was it too late to stop all of this? He could always swap the note with another one, saying 'FF does NOT want to go.' He got up off his bed and went straight to the front door, just as his dad was about to put his key into it.

'Well, that's what I call service,' he said.

'I was just about to go out.'

'Out? Where?'

'Grandpa's,' said Felix.

'That's funny. He usually lets me know.'

'Well, it was going to be a surprise,' said Felix, pulling at his jumper.

'When do you think I was born? Yesterday? I know what you're up to, you little liar.'

'I'm not, Dad. Honest.'

'Yes, you are. You're a little liar and you're not going anywhere.'

'But I've got to. It's really important.'

'What's really important?'

'Nothing, Dad.'

'No! Exactly! I'm going to double lock the front door and you're staying put, son.'

'Yes, Dad,' he said and returned to his room, wondering why everything that he did always ended up like this. He must have dropped off to sleep after that because the next thing he knew was that it was completely dark. But not just that. There was someone in his room.

'Oh my days! Who are you?' shouted Felix to this smartly dressed boy with neat hair and spectacles. 'What are you doing? Get out of my room **now**, or I'll call the police.'

'Oh, I'm sorry,' replied the boy. 'I didn't mean to wake you. I thought that you were expecting me though.'

'What do you mean? Who are you? What's happening? How did you get into my room?'

'Well, to answer all your questions in the order you asked them: firstly, I am your collector; secondly, I have come here to prepare you for your collection on Holloween;

and thirdly, I have arrived here through the window that is currently open between the planets Tritan and Earth at this auspicious time of year.'

'Oh, I see. I was going to put another note up to say that I didn't want to go to the party after all.'

'Which party?'

'The Holloween party.'

'Oh, no. It's not a party. It's a whole way of life.'

'For who?'

'For Sagacitors.'

'For what?'

'For Sagacitors. SAG-ASS-IT-OARS. Sagacitors.'

'Well, what do you mean – Sagacitors? I'm not a Sagacitor. I don't even know what one is.'

'Oh, I think you are – without even knowing it.'

'Am I? How do you know?'

'Show me your right ankle... Oh, yes. There's no two ways about that one.'

'What one?'

'Your birthmark. It couldn't be more perfect. You're definitely a Sagacitor. All Sagacitors have one of those until they're around fifteen. And then they disappear.'

'What is a Sagacitor then?'

'A Sagacitor is a person who lives for about 400 years and helps keep the world in check. Obviously, they can't stay in the same body for that length of time. So, they have to become a new person each time they die. If your mother was still alive, she might have dropped a few hints.'

'How would she have known?'

'Oh, because she was one too. Sagacitors sometimes give birth to other Sagacitors. They also have a tendency to be drawn to each other without even knowing it. If you come to Hollow Island, you'll find out much more about them.'

'But I don't want to go. It just sounds weird. And I can't risk it.'

'Very well. I can't force you. In fact, we have a strict policy of ensuring that all participants come completely of their own free will. I might try you again tomorrow, though, at about 11.45pm.'

'But I'll be asleep by then.'

'I won't wake you up. I promise. However, if you do change your mind... and we would love it if you did... perhaps you could stay awake, and we'll have another conversation then.'

'Well, I won't be awake,' insisted Felix.

'I'm sorry to hear that. But, as I said, I would never take anyone unwillingly. It's been a real pleasure to meet you, Felix,' he said and disappeared into the ether.

{ 2 }

Cold Feet and Hot Water

When his dad came knocking on his door the next morning, Felix was disappointed to find himself back in his boring old flat. The long, drawn-out dream that he'd been having had taken him to the rock face of Mount Everest, where he was centimetres from the top.

School was really boring that day. Jermaine was in

detention for both breaktimes. So, Felix decided to join in with the game of football that everyone else was playing. But when the ball was passed to him and he was about to shoot into an open goal, he got a flashback of the last time he'd done that. The time when he'd got so excited about scoring a goal that when he spun himself around to celebrate, he'd smashed Tyrone in the face with his arm and knocked him out cold. So, this time Felix just kicked the ball to hit the post instead. Everyone on his team was furious and he walked off.

'Going to any parties tonight?' said Edith as he passed her.

'No, my dad's girlfriend is cooking...Oh, I see what you mean. Um, I have been invited to one.'

'I told you. So, you are going?' she said, peering at him through her bright green eyes.

'Um...'

'It'll be really good. I promise you. You might even become a bit of hero there.'

'Yeah. A hero,' said Felix. 'Just like the one I am right now,' he muttered as he wandered off, staring at the ground and wondering whether she was a Sagacitor too.

On his way back to the flat after school, he dropped in on his grandpa's. Felix loved his grandpa. They'd talk about things that no one else would, except for Jermaine. They'd watch old black and white movies together and imitate the ridiculous accents that people used to have then. They'd talk in gobbledygook, and he'd do the best bad-grandad dancing that he'd ever seen. So, it was always great to see him, even though he was ill.

'Grandpa?'

'Yes, Felix.'

'I'm not being rude or anything, but can I ask you a question?'

'You can ask me whatever you like.'

'Well, I was just wondering. What do you think happens to people when they die?'

'Oh, goodness. Are you worried about me or something?'

'No, no. I didn't mean that. I just wondered what you thought.'

'What I think, what I've been taught and what I feel are three very different things. I don't know. I was brought up to believe that I'd go to Heaven if I was good and Hell if I was bad. But the more I think about it, I really don't know – which is why I've stopped thinking and let this,' he said pointing to his stomach, 'work it all out for me.'

'What? Your belly button?'

'Ah, no. The gut, silly!'

'Oh. Does your gut tell you where Grandma is?'

'Yes, it does as a matter of fact.'

'Where's that?'

'Somewhere else.'

'Where's that?'

'I don't know but she's not being burnt by coals or anything like that.'

'Good.'

'No. She's in another place and I don't know where that is. But what I do know is that she's happy.'

'What about my mum?'

'Oh yes,' said his grandpa. 'I think the sume. The same.'

'Does your belly button tell you that?'

'Yes. My belly button tells me that.'

They both laughed, but Felix didn't believe that his grandpa really felt that. He knew that he was just trying to be kind.

'Did she really not like me?'

'What are you talking about, boy? She loved you more than she ever loved anything.'

'But I was a difficult child, wasn't I?'

'No more than any other child.'

'But that's what killed her, wasn't it?'

'What?'

'My being difficult.'

'What makes you think that?'

'Oh. Nothing, really.'

'Is that what your dad's been...?'

'No, not exactly.'

'No...' But Grandpa, overcome with a coughing fit, was unable to continue. 'Anyway, you better get yourself back home,' he said eventually. 'Or you'll be late for your birthday dinner.'

'I will, Grandpa. Thanks again for the Fitbit. It's already come in useful,' said Felix.

'Probably much better than my watch, which always wants to stop. I wish this blooming cough would stop,' he said, but was unable to say anymore as the blooming cough did not look as though it was going to stop. So, Felix headed back to the flat.

As he got out of the lift, the smell from Lauren's cooking had already stunk out the hallway. She didn't seem to know anything about his mum's anniversary, which was strange because what she gave them was more like a death day meal than a birthday one.

'How old are you today, Felix?' she said, as she dished out her Coronation Chicken, full of bone and gristle, and covered in a sweet and sickly, yellowy sauce.

'Thirteen.'

'Oh. Happy Birthday, Son. I forgot to give you this. Here...' said Felix's dad, handing him a card with a picture of a birthday cake on it. Felix wondered why he couldn't have just given him the real thing for once.

After they'd finished eating, Dad suggested that he did the washing up while he fixed a chair that had broken when Felix had been sitting on it.

'Not in the dishwasher though. You can do it by hand,' he said.

'Oh. OK, Dad.'

As Felix went into the kitchen and started filling the plastic bowl with hot water, Lauren came to join him. So, that's what this was about. *Getting to know each other.*

'Everything alright at school today, Felix?' she said, picking up a tea towel.

'Yeah, a bit boring though, 'cos Jermaine's in detention all week.'

'Oh, what about all your other pals? They can't all have been in detention as well.'

'I don't really have any – to be honest.'

'I'm sorry to hear that, Felix. Now...' she said, inspecting one of the glasses that he had just handed to her. 'You haven't washed this one properly, have you. Well, at least I know it was mine, unless you've started wearing lipstick, that is.'

'No, Lauren. I haven't.'

They both laughed.

'And that fork's got bits of sauce on it. You know, you're not doing yourself any favours by not washing things properly. And forgive me, but if you don't mind me saying – that includes yourself. In the bathroom. Do you know what I mean?'

'I do,' said Felix. 'It's just that...'

'If you want to try and make some new friends, you should really do something about your personal hygiene.'

She was only trying to help. But it was bad enough having kids at school making comments about this all the time. He couldn't help it if his dad only washed his shirts once a month.

'Well, what do you want me to do?' he said. 'Cover myself in perfume like you do!'

He got a bit closer to her and took a sniff. And it was horrible. So horrible it made him gag and that, along with the revolting food she'd cooked, made him throw up – all over her dress.

For a moment, she didn't say anything but then she screamed. His dad dropped the chair and came running in to see what the matter was.

'What the hell's going on?' he said, looking at Lauren's dress.

'Get this disgusting stuff off me immediately,' she shouted.

And without even thinking, Felix picked up the washing up bowl with all its soapy water in and tried to splash some of its contents over her dress. Only it wasn't just some of it. It was practically all of it. This time, she stood completely still and there was silence, which Felix was the first to break.

'I'm so sorry. I didn't mean to...'

'Steven,' she said. 'Could you get my coat.'

And that was it. Off she went.

'Sorry, Dad.'

Silence. Neither of them moved a centimetre. His dad looked him in the eye, but Felix just stared at all the cracks in the wall behind him.

'Well, aren't I the silly one! What on earth made me think this was going to be a successful evening? True to form, everything you touch turns to ashes. You've got a bit of a habit of sending people packing on your birthday,' he said as he went into his bedroom. 'At least this time, it wasn't to their grave.'

And the door slammed behind him. So, Felix went into his room and lay back on his bed.

He'd apologised to both of them. And now he was being held responsible for his mum's death. Was he really? No one had ever told him how she had died. Whenever he asked them, he never got a clear answer. Did she take her own life? Was it because he was even more of a terrible two-year-old than most kids? The only person that could truthfully tell him was her – and she wasn't here to answer that. Maybe his dad was right. Maybe everything he touched did turn to ashes. So, he just stared up at the ceiling, wondering how he could make things better.

After a couple of hours, Felix heard his dad going out through the front door. Strange. The pubs would be closed by now. Then, about half an hour later, he felt as though something was in the room with him.

'Hello,' whispered Felix. There was no response, but the presence remained. It seemed like it was warm and friendly, so he wasn't worried.

And then at 23.45 precisely, the collector appeared like a hologram next to his wardrobe.

'Hello again,' he said.

'Oh! So, you have come back. Was it you that came ten minutes ago?'

'No.'

'You didn't send something ahead of you...or anything?'

'No.'

'Oh. Don't worry...'

'So, have you thought about what I said last night?'

'Well, not really. But you know you said that my mum was a Sagacitor.'

'Yes.'

'Does that mean she'll have moved on to being another person now?'

'Yes, she should have done. And she may well be among the new recruits going to Hollow Island this year. We won't know who she is yet though, of course. Not until she's been there to find out.'

'But she'll be two years younger than me, won't she?'

'Yes, but some kids start going from the age of ten.'

'Do you think I might be able to meet her if I went?'

'Well, if someone reveals themselves to have been her, you might well be able to meet them.'

'Oh, OK,' said Felix. 'Well, let's do it then.'

'Are you sure?'

'I couldn't be more certain.'

'Great. I'm Adrian by the way.'

'Hi, Adrian.'

'I do first need to remove some of the positive energy from the room though,' he said as he produced a whole lot of spinning objects out of his bag and set them into motion. 'These tops were forged out of a special metal called planium, which you can only find on Tritan and they bring out the negative energy in the room, which is what is needed to open up our point of entry.'

'OK.'

'So, if you just put some more clothes on over your pyjamas while I'm doing this.'

'OK.'

'...and then come over here,' said Adrian, gathering up his instruments.

'OK,' repeated Felix.

'Now, if you let me pick you up,' he said, putting one hand on Felix's back and the other on his legs, ready to scoop him up. 'And if you can keep as still as possible. You'll probably feel a bit sleepy. But don't worry. It's me that has to stay sharp and concentrated.'

SLEEPY! How could he possibly have been sleepy when

his whole body seemed like it had been laid out on an operating table with doctors and nurses at either end, pulling his arms and legs so tightly that all his limbs felt like they were eight-foot long. Within seconds however, he was out for the count.

{ 3 }

Hollow Island

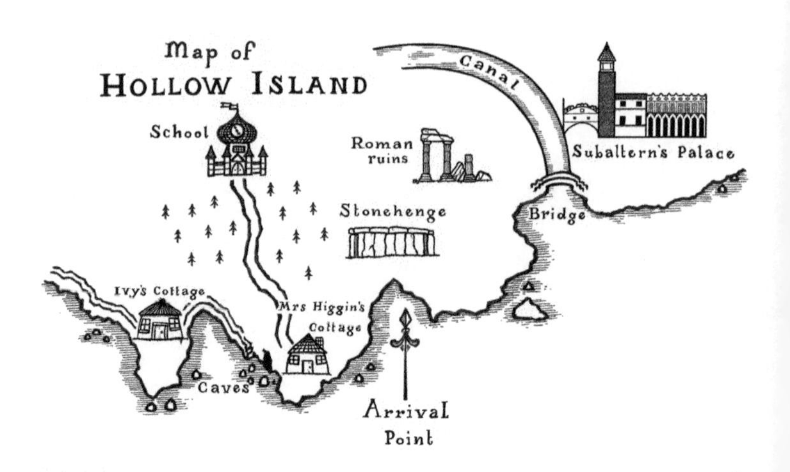

'OK. You can wake up now,' said Adrian, as they burst out of a vacuum in the sea and landed on a rocky shore.

'Is this Hollow Island?' said Felix, putting his feet down on the ground and rotating himself around – so that he could take it all in.

'Sure is.'

'I went on holiday to a place like this once.'

'Where was that?'

'Cornwall.'

In fact, it was even better than that. The rugged coastline and the crystal-clear water were the same, but up above him was this strange looking landscape, full of exotic plants, trees, flowers, and anything else that grew up from the ground. Birds were flying in perfect formations and a cluster of tiny insects glided along the cliff top, stretching itself out into an endless series of geometrical shapes before closing back up again. Down below, brightly coloured fish leaped out of the sea like a firework display. It seemed like all of nature was on a half-term break.

'But the wildlife is more extraordinary than it is there,' said Felix, as he breathed in the unpolluted air.

'Yes. It's all evolved here in its own rather peculiar way.'

'What, like that king-sized dragonfly,' he said, pointing up at an insect with multi-coloured scales. 'We don't have ones like that back home.'

'Nor here very often, actually. I've never seen one of those before. I think they're quite rare. Looks like it's been designed by Damian Hurst.'

'Oh, yeah. It's totally amazing.'

'It certainly wants to draw attention to itself. And it seems to have taken a liking to you.'

'Yeah, it does,' said Felix, as the thing kept flying towards him in a continuous loop the loop.

'Yes, it's dancing around all over the place.'

'So, it's daytime here at the moment?' said Felix, realising that he'd moved from darkness to light in a few seconds.

'Yes. Look at your Fitbit.'

He did. 1700 hours.

'It's the only bit of modern technology that works on this island. And that's because it would have corrected itself as it broke through the wall between the two worlds. There's nothing to guide it here though. No satellites or anything.'

'Aren't I supposed to be back home in six hours' time?'

'Yes, but... Sorry, Felix. I didn't tell you... Deliberately, actually... Because you might not have come otherwise. Every minute on Earth is a day on Tritan.'

'What?'

'So, you'll actually be away for...'

'360 days, which is nearly a year. A year!' he screamed.

'You stay here for a year and return at five past six, just before the wall hardens up again. Then everything goes into reverse. Every minute here for a period of approximately six hours and five minutes is a day on Earth. That's why everything has to be timed so precisely.'

'So, in other words, the two worlds get back in synch with each other.'

'That's right,' said Adrian.

'OK. OK,' said Felix. 'A YEAR!'

'Yes. And that...' said Adrian, pointing along the cliff to a large, old, rambling cottage, covered in climbing plants, '...is where your home will be for A YEAR.'

'If you say so.'

'I do. Anyway, you better go and introduce yourself to Mrs Higgins. She'll be getting a bit anxious and I'm behind schedule. Couple more people to pick up. Welcome to Hollow Island!'

'Cheers, Adrian,' Felix shouted back as he ran off towards the cottage. He took a quick look round to watch his friend do his disappearing act but managed to trip over a branch in the ground at the same time. Falling flat on his face, he looked up to see a very solidly built but upright woman, with her hair neatly tied up in a bun.

'You must be Felix Featherstone,' she said, over-enunciating every word. She had one of those accents that seemed like it might have started off as cockney but ended up more like Queen Elizabeth the Second's. 'I've put you into the Sea View room. Your fellow occupants thought that you'd appreciate it more than they would.'

'That is kind of you, Mrs Higgins,' said Felix, as he got himself up off the ground.

'It's not me that you should be thanking. It's these people,' she said.

'Jermaine!' exclaimed Felix as his friend appeared from behind the door. 'I don't believe it. Why didn't you tell me you were coming?'

'Why didn't I tell you? What you on about? You know what the score was,' said Jermaine.

'Yes, we were supposed to keep it a secret,' said Edith as she appeared too.

'And Edith as well! I thought as much. That's why you kept going on about Halloween parties. How did you know that I was a Sagacitor? ...Oh, yes. Of course. The birthmark.'

'Well, I'd better show you round the house, Master Felix,' said Mrs Higgins.

'Master Felix? Is this Dickens' Land or something?'

'No, but some of us more... how should I put it... more mature people here have decided to live a more old-fashioned type of life. I used to run a very respectable boarding house back at home. Rooms to let and that sort of thing. I ran a very tight ship, and my lodgers were all very respectful. Not like the ones you get in this day and age. You can live in the past here.'

And she led him into her cosy little kitchen, full of copper kettles, teapots, and old bits of china.

'Can't live in the past in TWAWKI anymore,' she said.

'TWAWKI?'

'Yes. *The World As We Knew It.*'

'But I thought that Sagacitors were *supposed* to go back to TWAWKI.'

'They are. But I'm not a Sagacitor. Nor are most people like me on this island. We volunteered to become part of the workforce, disappeared off the face of the Earth and then came here for a new life. But anyway, we can't stand here chatting all day. You should go and have a nice bath, Felix. You've had quite a journey. I must get on with the supper.'

Felix did as she suggested and soaked himself in a hot tub. As he came out of the bathroom, he saw the words 'Sea View' carved into the woodwork of the door immediately opposite him.

'I've put out a change of clothes for you on the bed,' Mrs Higgins shouted up the stairs.

It wasn't just fresh clothes though. It was fresh everything: towels, sheets, blankets – the lot, all smelling of spring. Felix got dressed, lay down on the bed and inspected his new environment: an old oak chest, a spinning top, a model theatre with actors on the stage, a bookcase, beams on the ceiling and the most spectacular view of the sea. His moment of tranquility was interrupted though by another call from downstairs.

'It's ready when you are, Felix. I've done a nice fry up.'

'It smells really good, Mrs Higgins,' he said as he went down into the kitchen.

'I do like to ensure that all my residents are happy. Do you want the full Hollowish?'

'Yes, please. Not too much bacon though.'

'Oh, no. We don't have bacon here. But we do have something which tastes like it. Trailcon. And these things, which bear a remarkable similarity to eggs, are called ovums. Oh, and of course we don't have mushrooms either. We have halooms. They're a different shape but they're just as nice.'

Everything was the complete opposite of what his dad had cooked him the other day. The trailcon melted in the mouth. The ovums had a texture which was neither rubbery, runny or phlegmy but more like mushrooms – or halooms as they were called here.

'This is so much better than anything we get back home,' said Felix.

'That's because of the environment. It's very pure here,' said Mrs Higgins.

'Is that why the colours of the trees and plants are so bright here?' asked Jermaine.

'Yes, it always reminds me of those films I used to watch back in TWAWKI, where everything was in technicolour.'

'Because there's not much pollution here,' said Edith.

'Yes, no global warming and all that sort of thing.'

Mrs Higgins reminded Felix of a teacher he had once had at primary school who, although she was very strict, made everyone feel safe and happy in the classroom. And her cooking was definitely the best he'd ever had. Just as he was mopping up the sauce on his plate, she stood up, put her hand in front of her mouth and did a 'Hep, hem'.

'Now, I don't want to alarm you, but I feel that it is my duty to give you a little word of warning. Hollow Island is a beautiful place and I've had the happiest days of my life here. However, just occasionally, we get a bad apple, a malevolent Sagacitor who tries to alter the way things are.'

'Is that happening at the moment then, Mrs Higgins?' said Felix.

'I'm not saying that it is and I'm not saying that it isn't. Only Mrs Butcher told me this morning that she'd walked past the barometer and that it was a light shade of pink, but her husband said that it was just her spooky imagination.'

'What barometer?'

'We have our own version of Stonehenge here and it acts as a barometer. If it stays its normal colour, it means that the energy on the island is good. If it changes colour and starts to go red however, we know that evil forces are at play or are on their way. It acts as a warning signal. And that's just what I'm doing to you. Anyway, I expect you'll be wanting to get to bed. You've all got school tomorrow.'

'School?'

'Yes, School.'

No one had said anything about SCHOOL! This was not what Felix had signed up for. It was bad enough trying to cope with SCHOOL back home, but to have to spend a year at another one – when he could just have been in bed asleep – was ridiculous. But then again this was a new chance – a new beginning.

School was a large Tudor Palace about half a mile's walk from the cottage up a footpath, which was more of a tunnel that had been carved out through some woodland. Its trees, or whatever they were, seemed to move and twitch in time with the three of them as they headed off up the path the next day.

Since none of them were talking, Felix could take everything in, like their new uniforms, which weren't really new – or uniform for that matter. They were all a bit ragged and grey. Felix thought they looked quite cool against the cartoon-like colours of the natural world that surrounded them.

As they came out of the tunnel, they looked up to see a beautiful building with octagonal towers on either side of it and a big clock in the centre with *Stonewood School for Sagacitors* written underneath it in gold lettering and *Founded:1570* below that.

The gigantic doors, more like gates, of the hall were open as they arrived and Adrian was standing outside, taking photographs of everyone with a 1950s camera, made from black plastic.

'Good morning. Good morning,' he said in between snaps. 'Get yourself a space in there if you can find one. You may have to do a bit of gentle nudging though.'

The place was packed with roughly three hundred kids, all aged between about 11 and 14, most of whom were chatting and chirruping away. A few, however, looked lost and isolated. Which one of them was Felix's mum? There was no way of telling, except that she had to be one of the younger ones. The sun, or rather their equivalent of it, was shining brightly through a huge stained-glass window onto their cranky uniforms, giving each one its own distinctive colour. Fragments of light also gave a ghostly glow to some of the wooden carvings, dotted around the walls. These were Sagacitors who had spent some time on the island and a lot of them Felix recognised.

At the far end of the hall were two staircases leading up to a gallery, which ran all the way around the side of it. There were twenty-four doors opening on to it, which is exactly what they did in unison when twenty-four members of staff appeared and looked down on them from up above. Everyone was immediately silent as a woman, holding a lantern and wearing a long black dress and a lace cap, came slowly down the gold-painted staircase – turning into a series of different people and ending up on the stage as a clean-cut, fresh-faced, young man with floppy hair and glasses.

'I would just like to say how blissfully happy I am this morning, not only to greet all of you Sagacitors – or

Springers, as you'll be called from now on – but also to have the honour of being your head teacher. And I thought it only right to give you all a taste of what is to come. Once you get to Year 4, you too should be able to walk up or down *The Sagacitor's Staircase*. You will be able to climb through all of your past lives until you get to your Starter one at the top.

'Now, you all come from a wide variety of religious faiths, backgrounds and beliefs. But we, at this school, do not pretend to have any answers. All we do know is that anyone who attends this institution is a Sagacitor. In other words, you have lived another life before this one. And the first thing we need to discover is what your last life was. And that is what we shall be doing today. Finding out what you have been in your other lives as a Sagacitor is imperative for your training. It's only then that you can start drawing on those qualities that you have had in the past and which, in this life, have been forgotten about. We will be utilising all of that and building on it...I shall now hand over the task of informing you where you are all to be placed to Mrs Snapdragon.'

A door at the back of the hall beside the stage was opened and they were led down the corridor, which seemed to go on forever.

'This way!' said the stooped and spindly Mrs Snapdragon, who had one of those voices that told you that she didn't put up with any nonsense from anyone or anything, whether it be a dog, a child, or a fellow guide. However, when she came to a standstill and looked back through her peering eyes at the three hundred pupils behind her, not a word needed to be spoken. Every single one of them looked like they knew what sort of behaviour she expected, and they got themselves into a perfectly straight line behind her. All chatter came to a stop.

'This door here, Springers, leads into Sage Class. Anyone who is a member of that class, please peel off and enter into it, as soon as I've called your name out.'

Once all the names from that class had been read out, which included Jermaine and Edith, the rest carried on walking down the corridor until they came to a halt at the next room. This stopping and starting continued until they finally reached Warrior Class, where Felix's name was eventually called out.

As he went into the classroom, Felix took a quick peek into the room at the very end of the corridor, which was called *The House for Lost Souls*. It looked just like one of those Victorian classrooms that he'd learned about at primary school. There was even a cane and a dunce's hat on the teacher's desk. He couldn't imagine what on earth they got up to in there. He was thinking that someone should report them. Beating kids and making them stand in the corner with a hat on their heads was definitely illegal and only happened in nightmares. But this was a **different** world and a **different** set of rules applied.

His class though was a bit like a Roman Arena, and Felix and his fellow Warriors were asked to sit in a circle around it.

'Good afternoon, Warriors,' said Mr O'Flaherty, as he welcomed them to his little kingdom. Felix couldn't work out whether it was his bow tie, his multi-coloured waistcoat or the gaps in between his teeth that stood out the most.

'This, I hope, will be a very auspicious day for all of you. No one,' he said, his eyes sparkling and shining as they took in each member of the group, 'will leave this room as the person that they came in here as.'

He left a pause here, just like TV presenters did when they wanted to keep you in suspense.

'I say this both literally – you'll see why in a minute – and metaphorically. Metaphorically, because you will see such things in this room as you have never seen before. The circle that you are sitting around is – dare I say it – a magical circle. When you step inside it, it is possible not just to relive but also to **become** one of your former selves. Now you may all be looking at me and thinking – "That's Mr O'Flaherty. We saw him earlier and he's exactly the same now." And how right you would be. However...'

Mr O'Flaherty stood very still and concentrated hard.

'If I allow myself to give in to my former self – which I won't do now – I could start to become... I think that you're getting the idea. So, if I could have a volunteer.'

Felix found that his hand went up almost involuntarily.

'Felix, that would be excellent. Come into the centre of the circle.'

He did so and Mr O'Flaherty swapped places with him – asking him to close his eyes and tell everyone what he was feeling.

'I can feel the biting wind blowing so hard against me

that... I must return to my tent and the warmth of my sleeping bag.'

Mr O'Flaherty threw a blanket over to him, which he covered himself up in.

'It's only when the wind starts to drop a bit,' continued Felix, but in a voice nothing like his own, 'that I am able to come out from my shelter.'

As he pulled back the blanket, everyone who was sitting in the circle around him let out a gasp. He had grown into this tall, strong man with an angular face and a New Zealand accent.

'I am hoping that today will be the day that man has finally reached the top of the highest mountain in the world. My fellow mountaineer, Tenzing Norgay, and I will set off to see if this is humanly possible.'

'But you're risking your life in doing this, Edmund,' interrupted Mr O'Flaherty. 'Why?'

'Because it is there and because, quite simply, I have to.'

A rope fell down in front of him and he grabbed it tightly with both hands. Felix climbed up it and through a hole in the ceiling until he'd disappeared. Once he was completely out of sight, Mr O'Flaherty called up to him.

'Thank you, Felix. We'll stop there.'

So, Felix reappeared, looking like he did when he'd first come into the room. The only difference was in his demeanour. Instead of being shy and anxious, he now appeared to be a bit more upright with his head held up in the air.

When the class was dismissed at lunchtime, Felix went back to the main hall, which had been turned into a canteen, loaded his plate up from the serving counter and joined Jermaine at one of the long tables.

'What you got there, Flix?'

'Theese and biscuits.'

'THEESE?'

'Yeah, that's what they call it here, apparently.'

'So, what have I got?' asked Jermaine, looking at him impishly.

'Chips , of course.'

'You mean: THIPS!'

'Oh, yeah. THIPS!'

They both laughed and got on with their meals.

'Have you had a go yet?'

'Not happening, Flix.'

'What d'ya mean?'

'It's not working. I've had a go, but nothing happened. I just stayed as Jermaine. Everyone else managed to do it. Edith turned into Mother Teresa from Calcutta.'

'Oh, cool. Yeah, I know. The one who used to look after all those people who were dying...No one was my mum, were they?'

'No, I don't think so, Flix. Sorry, mate.'

'That's all right. So, what are you going to do?'

'They're going to try again this afternoon. If that doesn't work, I might have to go home. Bit of a pity really 'cos I heard someone say it was **thops** tomorrow and they're my favourite, man.'

'Thops?'

'Yes, lamb thops.'

'What, with thips?'

'That's right, Flix. Thops and thips.'

'And then therry pie for afters.'

'Yes. And theddar theese and thutney.'

The clanging of an enormous hand-held bell brought an abrupt end to all conversations and everybody went silent. Mrs Snapdragon asked them to form an orderly line and each class returned to its room.

That afternoon, Felix watched a whole lot more incredible transitions, with kids turning into soldiers, rock musicians, nurses, and film stars from another time. One of the best moments was when Rohan became Martin Luther King and gave his *I had a Dream* speech. The one he made in 1963 where he dreamed about white kids and black kids mixing happily together and everyone being equal.

Felix kept secretly hoping that someone would turn into Judy Featherstone, but that never happened. It didn't matter though. He still had a great time.

'What an impressive assortment of Springers we have here,' said Mr O'Flaherty. 'This has been your first real opportunity to get to understand what Sagacitors do. Martin Luther King stood up for every black person in the world and fought for their rights. Rosa Parks did the same. Soldiers who committed extraordinary acts of bravery did so for their fellow countryman. Nurses like Florence Nightingale did as well. Edmund Hillary not only conquered Everest, but he was also a pacifist who kept bees. No one knew that these people were Sagacitors, but their influence has affected the way that huge numbers of others have behaved. No one must ever know who we are on TWAWKI, *The World As We Knew It*, but we must keep on doing what we have to do.'

There was a silence as they all took this in.

'And on that note,' said Mr O'Flaherty after a few seconds, 'you are free to go home, Warrior Class. I will see you all on Saturday. Tomorrow is a day off for you.'

As Felix left the room and walked down the corridor, he was distracted by something annoying buzzing round his head, which he tried to swipe away. Looking at it properly though, he realised that it was the dragonfly with multi-coloured scales that he'd seen when he had first arrived.

'Oh, blimey! Sorry.'

The insect did a somersault, flew back down the corridor, and then returned to its hovering.

'What's it doing?' he said to himself. 'Maybe it wants me to follow it.'

So, he did, and it flew a few more feet further forward. But then it started off again. So, he kept following it towards the door of The House for Lost Souls. Instead of hovering though, it flew round in a continuous halo-like circle above his head, giving him a bit more distance this time.

He couldn't work this out. Did someone want to see him for another session? Surely, they would have told him. Felix moved away from where he was to see if the insect would follow. It didn't but instead continued to circle above the exact same spot in front of the House for Lost Souls. Obviously, that's where he was supposed to be. So, he went back and stood there, wondering what on earth this could all be about until he heard a high-pitched male voice breaking through the silence.

'It's only on rare occasions that we are forced to resort to the methods that we have just employed,' said the guide. 'They were not meant to cause you any harm, of course – merely to put you into another state of mind. One in which you might think differently about who you are and who you were. A bit of a shock often does the trick. So, let's go through it again. You saw people being killed?'

'I think so,' said a voice that sounded like Jermaine's.

'Are you sure that it wasn't you that did the killing?'

'I might have done.'

'So, who were these people that died?'

'I'm not sure.'

'This is quite common, Jermaine. People who think that they might have attempted to kill someone in their last life are often in denial. In other words, they do not let themselves acknowledge the truth. But we must find out. Sagacitors are just as capable of becoming evil as anyone else.'

'Are you saying that I might be bad in this life?'

'I don't think so. But we must make absolutely sure. If it turns out you are, we will do everything we can here to help you turn this around and get you back on the right path again. It's in your own interest.'

So, Felix was a hero in his previous life, while his best friend might have been a murderer. This didn't make any sense. Jermaine was the kindest, gentlest, and most sensitive person that he had ever met. If anyone were to have committed a brutal act, it would have been Felix. He found it so difficult to keep a grip on his anger at times that he could imagine himself losing control and doing something that he regretted. But then that was not the same as murder.

He shuffled off down the hallway with speed and waited outside the school for Jermaine.

'Ah, well. That was good while it lasted,' said Jermaine, as they walked off towards the tree tunnel.

'What was?' said Felix.

'I'm off to the Palace tomorrow.'

'Which palace?'

'The Venetian Palace. It's where they send you if you've been a naughty boy.'

'But you haven't been...'

'Not in this life, but I have in the previous ones!'

'Jermaine, you are not a murderer. In this life or any others.'

'What makes you say that?' retorted Jermaine.

'Because I heard... I overheard your conversations. You can't give in to this, Jermaine. I know that your guide is wrong.'

'Do you?'

'Yes. Yes, I do. I swear. OK, you may have killed someone. Maybe you were in the army or something and you were just doing your duty. Listen, have you ever in your life worried about a feeling inside you that you can't control?'

'What sort of feeling?' he said, as they came out of the tree tunnel and into the open.

'Anger, for instance. Have you ever felt something so

strong inside you that you worry that it might lead you to do something terrible?'

'No.'

'I have.'

'Yeah, you can't control your anger. We all know that.'

'No, it's more than that. I sometimes worry that whatever it is that makes me feel the way I do is so strong that it will make me do something terrible. Not kill someone, but definitely hurt someone. Have you ever felt that?'

'No.'

'Well then, I am telling you that you are not a murderer.'

'Course I'm not. But what am I supposed to do?' asked Jermaine.

'I don't know. Maybe we should go and ask your collector. Do you know where your one lives?'

'Yeah. That cottage there. On the other side of the bay,' said Jermaine, pointing towards the next headland. 'But what good will he be?'

'Well, he might be able to stop you from going to that palace. You can't go there. That guide sounded well weird to me.'

'No, he's not.'

'Yes, he is. I'm telling you. Anyway, we can find out more from your collector.'

'OK!'

'Well, come on then. What are we waiting for?'

{ 4 }

Jo and Ivy

Fortunately, there was a light on downstairs in the cottage, where Jermaine's collector was living, and Felix peered through the window to check whether anyone was in. This was the type of place that he had only ever dreamed about, with its twisted beams, carved oak furniture and crackling log-fire.

'There's a couple of kids with long hair, sitting by the fire. Do you think that I should knock on the window?'

Jermaine took a quick look.

'Yeah, one of them's Jo. Go ahead and knock.'

A boy with shoulder length hair swivelled his head round and did a double take as Felix tapped on the glass.

'It's Jermaine... and Felix,' he called out in a muffled way.

'Hey, man. You gave me the shivers, man,' said Joseph as he opened the door. 'We don't normally get visitors at this time of night. Anyway, come in!'

'Sorry, Jo,' said Jermaine, 'but we need your help.'

'OK. What do you want me to do? Take you back home or something,' he said.

'Well, yeah. That's a good idea,' said Felix.

'Really?'

'Yeah, I suppose so,' said Jermaine.

'Oh, I was only teasing. You can't be homesick already.'

'No, but Jermaine's got to go to the Venetian Palace tomorrow.'

'Oh, I see. Do you have to, as well?'

'No, I'm alright. I've been identified as a Warrior,' said Felix with a little gleam in his eyes.

'Cool!'

'For me – yes. But not for Jermaine. It sounds really weird, that place.'

'And you want me to take him back?'

'Well, yeah. Something like that.'

'You don't understand, man. That would be like flying a private jet into Heathrow Airport without informing the flight controller. You've just picked the busiest time of year to do this. There's so much traffic coming in over the next few days.'

'Why's that?'

'Because there's all of the second, third, fourth and fifth years coming in over the next week.'

'Really?'

'Yeah, of course. This place isn't just for you Springers. You've had a head start of course because you're new, but there's also all of us lot as well, who want to continue our education. The only reason that I'm here early is because I'm a collector. Everyone else sets off from TWAWKI a few minutes later. It's all very tightly scheduled. I might be able to sneak you back in a week's time – our time, that is – when it all slows down again.'

'That'll be too late, though. Jermaine will be staying at the Venetian Palace by then,' said Felix, staring into the fire.

'Sorry, guys. It's totally beautiful at the palace though. It and the canal that leads up to it were built several hundred years ago by some mad poet, who was really into Venice, but who stopped coming to this island shortly afterwards. It's dead cool to look at with all its weird pillars, arches, and ornate carvings...'

'...And you get there by gondola,' said the girl with the cheeky face and the long dark hair, who had come over to join them.

'Oh, this is Ivy, by the way,' said Jo.

'Yes. And this is my house,' she said, doing a bit of a dance.

'You've got your own house?'

'Yeah, it's dead cool, isn't it? I'm in the second year and they've given me my own house.'

'That's extraordinary. No one would allow you to do that back in TWAWKI.'

'No, I know but they have...'

'...different rules here,' Felix cut in.

'Exactly. You've noticed,'

'Are you American?' said Felix, rubbing his chin.

'Yeah. Kind of.'

'And are you a collector?'

'No.'

'So how come you're here now.'

'Oh, I didn't bother to go back last year.'

'Oh. Wow! Your mum and dad must be well freaked out if you've been away for what...a whole year?'

'Maybe. They were probably quite relieved though. I didn't really think about it, to be honest. I was asleep for all of that time. It's only six hours here on Hollow Island. Anyway, I just love being here. I've got my own house. I can do what I want. Who would want to go back and live with their crumby parents?'

'So, do you know this palace?' asked Jermaine.

'Oh, yeah. I call it Sleepy Hollow because that's basically what it is. Mr Subaltern hypnotises all the residents and they walk around like zombies. And he treats them like slaves.'

'Does he use the cane and the dunce's hat, like he did with Jermaine?'

'Oh, yeah.'

'But that was only pretending,' said Jermaine.

'Because you weren't hypnotised. He knows that he can't get away with it if you're not.'

'That's bad. Why don't the guides stop him?' Felix chipped in.

'Because everyone – including the Head – is afraid of him.'

'So, what do we do?'

'Tomorrow, Jermaine will go to The Venetian Palace as planned,' said Ivy. 'He's got no choice. You, meanwhile, will do everything in your power to get him out of there.'

'Don't you worry. I will,' said Felix as they walked out of the door. That's exactly what Mrs Higgins had been talking about, he thought. Mr Subaltern must be this bad apple, this malevolent Sagacitor. He just hadn't expected it to be one of the guides.

Even though it was night-time, they could see quite clearly with two moons shining brightly down onto them. The air was still and the sea was lapping gently against the rocks as they made their way back to Mrs Higgins'.

'I wonder if you could...'

'What?' said Jermaine.

'I don't know. It's just wrong that you have to...'

'It'll be fine. Like everything else here. It may be a bit strange, but it's fine.'

'It doesn't sound like it will be. I'll come and check on you.'

'OK, Flix.'

'Do you think that this place has the same sort of... conditions as *The World As We Knew It* – TWAWKI. I mean there's the moons up there. OK, one more than we have, but they're similar – and there's a sun.'

'Only they don't call it the sun, they call it The Old Sol.'

'But we're the old souls,' said Felix.

'No, it's spelt differently: S-O-L. It's Latin for sun, apparently, and it's old because it's been around for twice as long as our sun.'

'But it's still similar.'

'Yeah, loads of things are. It's just the wildlife that's different. I think quite a lot of these animals were brought from TWAWKI hundreds of years ago. Then they acclimatised to this environment and evolved in their own peculiar way – like those weirdo creatures that have been following us. They're freaky, man. I mean most wild animals are either afraid of humans or they want to attack them.'

'Or they're just not interested,' added Felix.

'Yeah, but these ones have kept the same distance all the way. It's like they're spying on us or something.'

'No, I've never seen an animal behave like that,' said Felix as he watched what these long-necked, wolf-like creatures were doing. 'The people are quite similar though.'

'Course they are, Flix! The wildlife evolved here over hundreds of years, whereas all the people started their lives in TWAWKI, didn't they?'

'Surely some people were born here.'

'No, Flix. That never happens.'

'Why not?'

'Because they might be new souls and you can't have **new** souls going to a school for Sagacitors, can you?'

'No, you can't! That would be an outrage,' said Felix in a silly posh accent.

'Personally, I'm going to find it exceedingly difficult going back to school on TWAWKI, old chap,' said Jermaine, sounding even posher. 'Having to talk to and mingle with all those new souls that inhabit that ghastly place.'

'That's exactly the reason why I decided to stay on here,' called out a very superior voice from behind the front door of their cottage. 'Once you know what sort of people you mix with here, you don't want to have to reduce yourself to another level...And where have you two been, might I ask? It's way past your bedtimes, let alone the curfew.'

'Oh, sorry, Mrs Higgins. We just had to find out a few things because Jermaine's got to go to the Venetian Palace tomorrow.'

'Oh, that is a pity.'

'It's more than a pity. It's terrible. They don't treat people properly there. Do you know what they're really like, Mrs Higgins?'

'No, dear, I don't. I don't like to interfere. Anyway, you better get yourselves to bed. It's going to be quite some day tomorrow.'

'For Jermaine. Yes.'

'Do you want to take a bobolate up with you, boys?'

'Oh. Yes, please,' they said in unison.

When Felix got up to his room, he sat on the edge of his bed and sipped on his mug of hot bobolate – which was a tasty blend of marshmallows and chocolate. Looking around, he spotted a book on the shelf, called *The History of Hollow Island.* He found a chapter about how Sagacitors moved on after they had died. On Hollow Island, you learned how to hold onto your essence at the moment of death. And then how to transfer your essence to an unborn baby a few months before its birth. Sagacitors would sometimes wait many years before doing this and, quite often, they would choose to become the offspring of other Sagacitors. So that must have meant that he had picked out Judy Featherstone to be his mum. He wondered what it was that made her so special. If only he could meet her.

{ 5 }

The Venetian Palace

When Felix came down the stairs the next morning, there was no one else around. So he helped himself to breakfast.

'Well, we won't be seeing that young gentleman for a while,' said Mrs Higgins, as she came into the kitchen and started to busy herself with saucepans and tea towels.

'Has he gone?'

'Yes, someone came to collect him early this morning.'

'What, a collector?'

'No, no. Not in the sense you mean anyway. Just somebody from the palace – the ferryman.'

'Have you ever been into the Venetian Palace, Mrs Higgins?'

'I've gone past it many a time, but I've never been in. At the end of every year, we get taken on a bit of a cruise up the canal. It's a lovely day out. Now, it's a lovely day out today. You mustn't waste it. You should go and explore.'

'I will, Mrs Higgins.'

'I'll deal with the dishes. Now, off you go and enjoy yourself.'

As Felix walked up through the tree tunnel, a big cuddly ball of fur came bounding up to him. With its thin stripy head, it looked a bit like a badger, but with longer ears and longer legs. When it rolled over in front of him as if it wanted him to tickle its tummy, Felix bent down to stroke it. But the creature turned on him, biting his hand first and then scarpering.

Blood was pouring out of his fingers, so he went up to the school sanitorium.

'You're lucky that it's only as bad as it is,' said the kindly matron, who was washing his wound and then bandaging each finger up individually.

'Was I?' said Felix as he peered through the door of her office into the sick bay to see ten metal-framed beds on a polished, wooden floor.

'Yes, those Janus-facers can have your finger off if you're not careful,' said the matron, as she finished dressing his wounds.

'It looked like it was so nice though. You have to be really careful who or what you trust on this island, it seems.'

'Yes, you do,' she said.

'At least rats and snakes and tarantulas don't pretend to be nice.'

'Exactly. Anyway, you go and enjoy the rest of your day.'

'Where is the canal, miss?'

'Oh, you can't miss it, dear. If you head along the cliff path going east, you'll get to it eventually. But don't go stroking any more animals, Felix.'

'I won't, miss,' he said and ran out of the building, down the tree tunnel and along the cliff path.

When he got to the place where he'd first arrived on Hollow Island, he paused for a moment, sat down, and tried to remember what he had felt like then. So much had happened in the last three days, which back home in TWAWKI was only three minutes. Only three minutes had passed on TWAWKI since he'd left! The time it takes to make a cup of tea.

He glanced back behind to see five or six of the long-necked, wolf-like creatures – the ones that Jermaine and he had been followed by the night before. It was like playing grandmother's footsteps. Every time he looked round, they stopped still and pretended that they were minding their own business.

As he set off again, he passed a huge Victorian wool mill, a medieval castle, an empty hotel, and lots of timber-framed houses. Sagacitors had, of course, been coming here for years. Beyond all of that, he climbed through the remnants of a Roman village and past their version of Stonehenge – which was much greener than it was red...or pink. And then he saw the canal. And the palace, which looked even better than he thought it would, with its rows of arches on every level and ornate carvings – all reflected in the water directly in front of it. He didn't think that he had ever seen anything so beautiful. But perhaps Mr Subaltern's whole reason for having this palace was, as Ivy had said, to seduce you into thinking that it was a good place.

An old dilapidated bridge led to a fenced off area on the other side. There was no point in attempting to get to the palace that way. He'd have to go by boat. So, he went up to the gondola that was moored at the end of the canal. A big, beefy, old man was lounging inside it. Although he was wearing a hood over his head, Felix could still see his long grey beard and the bulbous eyes that were staring out at him.

'Excuse me,' said Felix.

'Yes,' replied the man.

'Is it possible for me to get to the palace?'

'Not unless you've been requested, no.'

'I just wanted to visit my friend.'

'What's his name?'

'Jermaine...Jermaine Toussaint.'

There was no response except for the fact that the ferryman, with his long wooden punt, pushed the boat out into the water and headed off in the direction of the palace. Felix looked back out to sea and watched a flock of thirteen yellow birds, gliding alongside the coastal path in a 1–2–4–6 formation, shaped like a triangle. He'd never seen that on TWAWKI. As the leader flew towards a tree and perched herself on a branch, the others followed suit, six landing on one side of her and six on the other. Why couldn't humans be as in tune with each other as that?

He turned back to see the old man returning with what looked like an empty boat. However, as he tied it up to one of the poles, Jermaine appeared from underneath an oil skin.

'Alright, Flix,' he said as he stepped onto the bank.

'Can we...?'

'What?'

'Go for a walk or something.'

'Oh, yeah. Sure,' said Jermaine with a giggle, as they wandered out of earshot of the ferryman. 'He's alright.'

'Really! What time's he knock off?'

'Six o'clock.'

'Great! I reckon that if I come back in a couple of days' time – at night – that you could swim down the canal to here, where I'll be waiting for you. Then we could get you back to Jo's and he could take you home.'

'But why would I want to do something like that?'

'To get out of here, of course.'

'Oh, I see.'

'You can't stay here,' whispered Felix. 'You heard what Ivy said about Mr Subaltern. He's evil.'

'No, I...'

'Well, he may not seem to be at the moment. But he...'

'No, he's cool, man.'

'But he beat you with a cane.'

'No. That was just pretending, Flix.'

'Didn't sound like it was. What were those 'methods' that he'd just employed...?'

'That was just talk. You weren't there, man. He's cool. OK.'

'Jermaine. You can't stay here. You have no idea what could happen to you if you stay. You're just being seduced into...into a false sense of...'

'Security? No, I'm not. It's going to be good for me...'

'I'm coming back again,' said Felix.

'Do as you please. I'm not leaving though, not until I'm ready, Flix. Understand!' said Jermaine as he walked back to the gondola.

'But that's going to be too late. Don't you understand? You idiot!' said Felix, grabbing his collar.

'What did you call me?'

'Sorry. I was just getting...'

'Angry. I know,' said Jermaine.

'Ok. I'll see you in a few days' time then.'

'OK. Anyway, got to go back in now.'

'Is this all the time they let you out for?'

'No, of course not. I can come and go as I please,' said Jermaine.

'So, why have you got to go in so quickly?'

'To finish my game of thess.'

'THESS? What's thess?

'You know. The one with a king, a queen, a bishop and some pawns.'

'Oh, THESS!'

'Yes, THESS!'

Felix laughed.

'Who's winning this game of thess?' he called out, as Jermaine got into the boat.

'Who do you think?' Jermaine said with a smile on his face as he disappeared back down the canal towards his grand, majestic residence.

At least his best friend still had a sense of humour. But that did not prevent him from being brainwashed. Jermaine's abrupt response to Felix's mention of the cane was, in Felix's mind, a complete give-away. There was no doubt that Mr Subaltern had beaten or at least threatened Jermaine with a cane. He'd heard what he'd said!

{ 6 }

Temper Tantrums

As soon as Felix got to school on Saturday, he found himself a space in the crowded hall and waited, as usual, for the head teacher to appear. Although he was surrounded by people, there was no one around him that he knew. So, he just stood there, looking straight in front of him.

'Hey, guys. Look who it is. The man who thinks that he's a hero,' called out a voice from behind him.

'Oh yes. It's the one who did none of the hard work but took all the glory,' said another.

'What do you mean?' said Felix.

The two boys came and stood either side of him, looking like a comedy duo. Sanjay was small and skinny, like Felix. George was the opposite.

'There were fourteen other people on that expedition, and they all got as close as they could to the top,' said Sanjay. 'It was just that one of them, and his Sherpa who he couldn't have done it without, pushed his way past everyone else and...'

'What you talking about? That's not how it was,' exclaimed Felix.

'You mean that that's not the way that you choose to remember it,' said George.

'No.'

'Can't wait to find out who you were before that. Probably some big fraudster or something,' said Sanjay.

Felix didn't have a chance to answer as the head teacher was making his entrance down the main staircase and the whole assembly had gone quiet.

He told them all about the Day of Revelation, his favourite moment of the week – if not the term. Many of them would be wondering how they could possibly find out who all their previous incarnations were – just in one day? The answer was, of course that once you knew what your last life was, you could probably find out from the records what all the other ones were before that, as you would almost definitely have been to the island many times before. So, the school could work out from that what their Starter Lives were.

Felix looked up at the three-dimensional carvings on the walls. They seemed to be peering down at them as if they were trying to spot which one of the pupils they had now become. Who here in this hall had been Mahatma Gandhi or Mrs Pankhurst in one of their previous lives? Today was the day to find out.

'Felix Featherstone! Room 21, please,' called out one of the guides from up above.

He followed his fellow pupils up the staircase onto the balcony and looked in through the doors at all the guides, who seemed more mysterious – and stranger – than any of his lot. Room 21 was closed. So, he had to knock.

'Come in!'

A woman in a wheelchair was in there, not the man who had called out his name. She seemed to be looking up at the ceiling.

'Hello, Felix.'

'Hi.'

'My name is Asha, and I am going to be your personal guide today. Have you settled in yet or are you still suffering from first-week-itis?'

'No, I've settled in.'

'We need the truth, Felix.'

'What do you mean?'

'I mean that here on Hollow Island, if we are to make any progress, we need to know what you are really thinking and what you are really feeling as well. Don't worry. You're not alone. Everyone has that problem when they first arrive. Where you come from, you almost have to tell half-truths in order to survive.'

'Yes, you do.'

'At least you are aware of it.'

'Well, I wouldn't be here if I'd told the whole truth back at home.'

'No, you wouldn't, because your dad and your school would have prevented your journey from happening if they'd known.'

'Yes, they would. My mum wouldn't have done though – if she was alive – because she must have been here herself.'

'Yes, she must.'

'And she might even be here now as a different person.'

'Indeed, she might. You'll have to wait and find out though.'

'But surely someone must have done just that. Found out that they were her. Can't you just tell me?'

'If they are here, we must allow **them** to tell you. I'm sure they will in good time. Now, we need to discover who you were in your Starter Life, the one which qualified you to become a Sagacitor. But I'm afraid it's all a bit worrying.'

'What is, miss?'

'Your records. They're worrying, but they're also somewhat confusing.'

'Are they?'

'Yes, they don't really make any sense. You found out with

Mr O'Flaherty that you had definitely been Edmund Hillary. Is that right?'

'Yes.'

'Yes, that's what Mrs Snapdragon thought. She read out your records to me this morning. I'm not going to tell you what they said. That will only make things worse than they already are. And I want to look into this.'

'But what sort of things does it say? Has it got something to do with my anger issues?'

'Your anger issues?'

'Yes, I get angry, and I can lose control.'

'Oh, that's a pity. Sagacitors bring peace to the world, not anger. However, if that's all that it was, it wouldn't be a problem. You can overcome anger. No, it's other things.'

'What kind of other things? This doesn't make any sense. Something weird is going on here. Edmund Hillary was a good man. Mr O'Flaherty said so.'

'Well, I will...'

They were interrupted by a knock on the door though.

'Could you get that?'

Felix opened the door to find George and Sanjay, the boys who had been teasing him earlier, standing there, like a picture of innocence.

'Excuse me, miss. I'm so sorry to interrupt you but the head teacher has asked to see Felix Featherstone,' said George.

'Oh yes, of course. You better go with them then, Felix. I'll see you later,' said Asha.

Felix welcomed this opportunity to see the headteacher. Perhaps they might get to the bottom of what was going on with his records. He shut the door behind him and followed the boys along the gallery until they got to the staircase.

'Oh, he gets angry, does he? – The Pacifist!' whispered Sanjay into his ear.

'We better be careful that we don't rub him up the wrong way then,' said George.

'No, we don't want him getting into a temper tantrum with one of us.'

'Have you been listening?' asked Felix.

The boys sniggered.

'Hang on. Have I really got to go and see the head teacher?'

The boys sniggered again.

'What are you playing at? What's your problem? You don't even know me. What have I done to you to make you want to do this to me?'

'Existed, mate. Existed,' said George.

'Why...are...you doing this...to me?'

'Oh, perhaps you should go back to Mummy. She'll kiss you better,' said George.

'But Mummy's not here,' said Sanjay. 'Do you want me to kiss you? There, there, my poor little diddums.'

The other one pretended to be *Mummy*, put his arms around Felix and rubbed his hand under his chin. It felt all bumpy because he had a wristband with an emerald stone on it. Felix decided not to give them the pleasure of letting them know that he didn't have a *mummy* though. Or, at least, if he did – that she was **here**!

There was no stopping Felix now. He grabbed hold of

one of George's wrists, which also had a wristband on, and thrust him away. The push was enough to send him a few yards down the corridor and George 'accidently-on-purpose' collapsed onto the floor. As this happened right at the top of the stairs, however, he went tumbling down them, hitting his head as he got to the bottom.

Felix didn't call out: 'How the lowly have fallen!', but he said it to himself. In the meantime, everyone had come out of their rooms to find out what all the noise was about. Mrs Snapdragon arrived at the scene just in time to see Felix standing at the top of the stairs, with his head held high, whilst his supposed victim was writhing in in agony below him.

'Felix Featherstone,' she called out. 'House for Lost Souls. **Now**!'

'Sit down,' she snapped as she led him into the disturbing room.

'Whereabouts, miss?' he said as he eyed all the Victorian benches.

'Wherever you like,' she answered.

'Yes, miss,' he said, sitting down directly opposite her desk, his shoulders tightening up and his posture stiffening.

Not a word was uttered for the next five minutes. Felix looked up into space whilst Mrs Snapdragon read through his notes. It felt like being at the doctor's.

'So, Felix,' she said eventually. 'You should by all accounts remember this place.'

'Yeah, I took a quick peek when we passed it yesterday.'

'I don't mean then. I mean in your previous incarnations.

According to your notes, you have been a frequent visitor and in fact were one of the first occupants just after it was built.'

'When was that?'

'In Victorian times, of course.'

'Oh, yes. Of course.'

'This is all very worrying. I had given you the benefit of the doubt. I had thought there was something wrong with your records. It is hard to imagine that Sir Edmund Hillary was a troubled student or that he had to go to the Venetian Palace. But after what has just happened, I have no other option than to believe what is written in your notes.'

'Yes, miss.'

'According to your records, all your previous lives – with the exception of your last one and your first one, of course – have been extremely disturbing. Strange that you should have had such an exemplary existence last time round. That's almost unheard of. Sagacitors change by degrees. A complete turnaround is almost impossible, which does make me think that someone's tampered with your records. Either that or there must have been darker things going on with Sir Edmund Hillary than the world ever got to hear about.'

She stopped and looked at him as if he should have been able to answer this.

'Well, were there?'

'I don't know, miss... But if they were so bad, why was I allowed to keep coming back? And surely the school would have done everything they could to help me? I don't know anything about the lives that I had before Edmund Hillary...'

'You will in good time. We'll take you through them,' she said, looking Felix straight in the eye. 'Hollow Island is generally a happy place. It has been used over the years to enable people to find the true depths of who they really are. We bring out the best in people here, in order that they can return to TWAWKI and perform their duties as Sagacitors. But just occasionally we come across a Sagacitor who has decided to change their ways. Some of them see reason and become good again. If your records are to be believed, this might be what happened to you in your last life. Now you must prove it in this one. Otherwise, there will be no possibility of you continuing here. You'd be too much of a risk. Anyway, you'll go back home now to Mrs Higgins, get your stuff and then you'll be taken to the Venetian Palace.'

'But that's evil.'

'What makes you say that?'

'People have told me that. Its beauty on the outside covers up the corruption on the inside.'

'Well, I don't know who you've been talking to but they're just trying to scare you. Now get back to Mrs Higgins' and I'll send someone to collect you within the hour.'

None of this added up. Someone had tampered with his records and the two boys had wound him up for no reason at all. At least he now had an opportunity to find out what was really going on at the Venetian Palace though. And, more importantly, this was his chance to get Jermaine out of there.

Mrs Higgins wasn't in when he returned, but the creepy

looking ferryman, dressed in black today, was waiting outside the front door.

'Are you here to take me to the palace?'

'That's right,' said the man, without even looking at him.

'I'll be with you in five then.'

'Make sure it's no more than that.'

'It won't be, sir.'

There was an old leather suitcase in Felix's room – just the right size for the few belongings and clothes that he had accumulated since he had been on Hollow Island. Having thrown everything in that he thought that he would need, he ran down the stairs and out of the front door.

'Alright. Let's go,' said the man, as he marched off along the cliff path past all the old buildings that Felix had seen the day before. As they walked on, Felix glanced back behind him to see some more of the long-necked, wolf-like creatures that he and Jermaine had been followed by the other night.

'Excuse me,' he said to the old man, who just stopped and looked at him as if he was waiting for his question. 'What are those long-necked wolves called?'

'Wolveraffes. They do everything in packs. Except when they're dead, of course. Found one by the canal yesterday. Never seen such a glossy, pristine coat. All those different patches of colour too. Must be twenty odd shades of brown. Beautiful when they've left this world. Nasty when they're still here though. Just ignore them.'

As they walked on, they passed the recreation of Stonehenge which, although it wasn't blood red, was definitely looking pinkish. This was bad. It made Felix realise that it wasn't just schoolboy arguments that were going on. There was something disturbing happening and the barometer had picked it up. Felix wanted to ask the ferryman, but he had that face which said that he'd told him quite enough already. He clearly wasn't prepared to say any more. Felix looked back to see if the wolveraffes were still following. They seemed to have disappeared, but there was a young boy, slightly darker skinned than Jermaine, who was doing a worse job of attempting to look innocent than the eery creatures had.

One moment, he'd pretend to be playing a game of jumping back and forward across a stream and then, as soon as Felix turned his back, he could tell that he'd be stopping and staring at him. Every time he looked round again, the boy would try and return to his stupid game, but he'd miss his footing and end up in the stream.

Everywhere Felix went, he was being stalked. But by who? Who were the animals and this boy working for? He couldn't believe that he was in this situation, which belonged in a world of espionage. It's not something that kids did – spy on each other! It was even weirder to think that animals were doing it as well.

{ 7 }

Brain Washing

'Right. Jump in,' said the grey-bearded man, as he held on to the end of a gondola.

Felix took his place, and just sat and listened as the ferryman's punt dipped slowly into the water and the squelchy mud below. When the palace came into view, it looked even better than before. What on earth lay behind all those windows though, he was about to find out.

Once the gondola had been tied to a post, Felix climbed out onto the palace forecourt and through one of its arches. No sooner had his feet touched the ground than the ferryman unhitched the rope and was off back down the canal again.

The front door opened a fraction and all he could make out was a pair of eyes staring straight out at him.

'Hello.'

'Oh, hello,' replied Felix.

'Can we help you?'

'Yes, I've been sent here by Mrs Snapdragon.'

'Name?'

'Felix Featherstone.'

'Come in. Someone will show you to your room in a minute.'

'I'll do that,' said a voice, which he immediately recognised.

'Jermaine!'

'Yes. I heard you were coming. Follow me!'

Jermaine grabbed his suitcase and headed up a stone spiral staircase, which seemed to go on forever.

'I hope everything is to your satisfaction, sir. Any problems, just ring for room service.'

'Room service?'

'Indeed, sir. As soon as you are ready, Mr Subaltern will see you in his office. When you have finished with him, perhaps you would care to join us in the Billiards Room for a glass of sherry, followed by a little bit of a knockabout.'

'A glass of sherry? Are you kidding me?'

'That is merely the term that the residents use for it. It does, however, taste like sherry – rich, thick, and fruity but without the alcohol.'

'Jermaine, what is this?'

'This is the Venetian Palace, sir. We look forward to your company in the Billiards Room. In the meantime, we hope that you enjoy your stay,' said Jermaine as he pulled the door shut behind him.

Felix started to unpack but was more confused than ever. Was this his friend play-acting as he often did or was this his friend being made to believe that he was living in some kind of grand hotel? It was hard to tell, but Felix didn't have much time to think about it as he was interrupted by a knock on the door.

'Felix!' called out a voice.

'Yes.'

'Mr Subaltern wants to see you in his office in five minutes.'

'OK. Where is it?'

'Two floors down.'

He had been summoned by the man himself.

The door of the office was open, so he walked straight in. Mr Subaltern was sitting at a large antique desk with a view of the canal behind him. The room was dimly lit, and he could only really make out that the man was small and skinny – and had a sweaty forehead.

'Ah, Felix,' he said in his high-pitched voice as he jumped up to shake hands with him. 'Welcome to the club.'

The club? He didn't like the sound of that. 'Thank you,' was all he could think of saying in response.

'I'm delighted you're here. You're a very curious case and I do love a challenge.'

'A challenge? Me?'

'Yes. We've never had anyone like you before. It's going to be fascinating to get working on you.'

'What did he mean – get working on me?' thought Felix. This was even more sinister.

'Get working on me?'

'Yes, to find out about what went wrong in those previous lives of yours.'

Why on earth would he believe that that was what he was going to do? Particularly after what Ivy had said.

'When will you start doing that?' he said, trying to stop his shoulders from twitching.

'As soon as you're ready. We'll give you a couple of hours to settle in, get to know the gang and the routine here and then... Oh, I gather that you've already got a friend here.'

'Yes. Jermaine Toussaint.'

'Yes. He's only been here a couple of days, but he's responding very well to the therapy.'

'Is he?' said Felix. 'Do I have to have this therapy?'

'No, of course not. You're here on Hollow Island of your own free will. We can't make you do anything. If you want to go back to TWAWKI, well then – so be it! However, I would strongly advise that you went through with our treatment programme. It has fantastic results – not just for here but also for when you return home. You'll be bringing back the elixir all right.'

'Bringing back the elixir?'

'Yes. It's a phrase used in mythology. In your case, it means that you'll be taking back something rich and empowering when you return to TWAWKI. However, if you were to return now...'

'Oh, I see.'

'Well, it's been good to meet you properly, Felix. I've heard so much about you,' said Mr Subaltern, as he shook hands with him. 'I suggest that you go and join the other reprobates now for a bit of...I don't know...whatever high jinks they're currently up to.'

'Thank you, sir,' said Felix as he left the room.

'Oh, leave the door open. I like to keep an eye on what's going on,' said Mr Subaltern with a bit of a chortle.

'Yes, sir.'

No one had told him where anything was. So, he went off to explore. Downstairs on the ground floor, most of the doors were open, so he could see what his fellow 'reprobates' were up to. Some were reading, some playing chess or Monopoly whilst others were drinking sherry, as they called it, and having a game of billiards. He liked the calm atmosphere. He always liked silence. But this was a different type of silence. It was really odd. What had Mr Subaltern done to all of these kids to make them behave like this? These guys seemed like they'd been zombified.

Felix felt the urge to jump up and scream, just to see if

he could get a reaction out of them. But no! What was more important was to get Jermaine out of here. Now! Before it was too late. Before anything was done to him. He couldn't see any sign of him down there, so he headed back up the stairs – past Mr Subaltern's office.

'Can I help you, Felix?'

'Oh, no. I'm alright.'

'You look lost.'

'No, I thought I might go back to my room. I haven't unpacked properly yet.'

'Have you brought a trunk or something?' said Mr Subaltern.

'No, just a small suitcase.'

'Well. I'm sure that that can wait. If you don't want to mix with your fellow inmates, perhaps we should get started on your therapy.'

'Alright,' said Felix.

'So – to begin with – we all know what your last life was. At least, every member of Warrior Class does.'

'Yes, they do.'

'But what about the one before that?'

'I've no idea, sir.'

'No, of course you've no idea. The notes in your file may be correct, but they may also have been tampered with. So, we need to try and find out by some other means. It's almost impossible to automatically return to the 'life before last' without some prompting. But it is essential that we revisit it. Until we do, we can't train you up to be a fully-fledged Sagacitor. A Sagacitor whose intentions are evil is can do an awful lot of damage in the world...Now I'm going to give you some...'

So, Subaltern wanted to put him into a trance like everyone else. There was no way that he could rescue Jermaine by staying in the palace. That would have to be done from the outside. But how could he get out? A temper tantrum, of course! They usually worked. Not the type that he'd supposedly had with George and Sanjay, but just enough of one to be a nuisance and to disturb the calm that chillingly crept throughout the building. It would not be difficult for him to have an outburst and create a scene. He was angry enough as it was – just being in this situation.

'Actually, I think that I would like to go and join the 'reprobates' after all.'

'Oh, good. I'm not going to stop you.'

He went back down the stairs and made a bee line straight for the Billiards Room, where Jermaine was just picking up a cue.

'Good timing, Flix. Fancy a game, old chap?'

'Thanks, old boy,' said Felix in his posh voice, playing along with his friend, but still worried about his state of mind. 'Could we play Monopoly instead though?'

'If that's what you want. Grab yourself a sherry.'

They sat down at the table with a few of the others, who were all – in Felix's mind – ridiculously obedient and well behaved. Not one of them was leaning back on their chairs in a chilled manner or rabbiting away to their mates. Kids could be quiet at times, but not like this. There was something almost **too** well-behaved about them, as they counted out the shares of money and dealt out the cards. Felix was more concentrated than he had ever been though. It was going to be a difficult game to play. On one level, he had to look as though he wanted to win whilst, at the same time, he needed to make a move which would lose him all his money. Half an hour into the game, he was four places away from Park Lane, where Jermaine had put two of his hotels. Here was his chance. He just needed to fix the dice when no one was looking.

'Actually, I think I might have another one of those sherries.'

'OK, I'll get you one,' said Jermaine.

Felix dropped a couple of his cards under the table.

'Don't worry. I'll pick that up,' said Georgia.

'Oh, thanks,' he said, making sure that his foot was firmly on top of them.

'Felix, your foot's on the cards,' called up Georgia from underneath the table.

'What was that?' said Felix, bending down to speak to her and 'accidentally' sending a glass of sherry flying, which went all over Dryden's shirt and trousers.

'Watch what you're doing!' exclaimed Dryden.

'Oh, sorry,' said Felix, taking the opportunity to make a fake throw. 'Two and two. Four!'

Felix placed the dice on the table and took his foot off the cards.

'But you didn't throw the dice,' said Dryden who was trying to get the sherry stain out of his shirt.

'Didn't I?'

'No, you just put them down.'

'Oh, sorry. I'll do it again,' said Felix, putting his foot back down on the cards. 'Oh, why don't you go and get a cloth from Mr Subaltern while I have my go.'

'Oh, yeah. Good idea,' said Dryden.

'Oh, no,' cried out Felix as Dryden left the room. 'I've got four again. One, two, three, four...Park Lane.'

'Brilliant. That's one thousand five hundred pounds, please,' said Jermaine, returning with the sherry.

'But I haven't got that much.'

'Well, you'll just have to sell some of your properties.'

'That's going to leave me with nothing. That's completely ridiculous. I hate this stupid game,' screamed Felix, throwing the board into the air with everything that was on it, just at the moment that Dryden returned – with Mr Subaltern.

'Felix Featherstone. My office!'

'Yes, sir.'

Mr Subaltern swivelled round and returned back down the corridor. Felix followed immediately behind – looking like a dog that had just been caught eating all the crisps. As he passed through the door, however, he turned back to the assembled company and stuck his tongue out as far as it would possibly go.

'Could you explain exactly what you hoped to achieve with this outburst?' said Mr Subaltern as he shut the office door behind him.

'I got frustrated, sir. I got angry.'

'And were you happy with this?'

'No, sir.'

'I would have thought that having been sent here for that very reason, the least you might have done would be to rein it in a bit.'

'I know, sir,' said Felix.

'It worries me to think that I might have had to have sent you over the bridge.'

'What's that, sir?'

'Over here, Felix,' said Mr Subaltern, taking him out of the office and pointing at a corridor, with windows either side, which went over the canal. 'We call it the Bridge of Sighs.'

'Why's that, sir?'

'Because it leads to the old cells and dungeons. Like the one in Venice, it was originally built as a passage between a palace and a prison. The convicted men and women sighed as they crossed it. In days gone by, they didn't just lock people up down there, they executed them as well.'

'You don't do that now, do you?'

'Of course not, Felix. But we do have occasion to put people down there for a few hours to cool off.'

Felix couldn't work out which was worse – the therapy or the cells.

'However, I've just had a call from the school. Apparently, George and Sanjay have admitted to being highly provocative towards you. They say that they staged the whole incident. So, they have accepted full responsibility for what happened today. In fact, they're not sure what had come over them.'

'No, sir.'

'In the light of that, the school will accept you back.'

'Thank you, sir.'

'You would get much more concentrated therapy here than you would there when it comes to approaching your past lives. And – according to your records – there is a lot of work to do. So, the choice is yours.'

'I think I'll go, sir,' said Felix, clenching his stomach muscles.

'Very well. The ferryman awaits.'

'Thank you, sir.

{ 8 }

Battle Plans

Once he'd been dropped off at the end of the canal, Felix dashed over to Ivy and Jo's to tell them about the palace. As he got close to the cottage, he heard a clacking sound, coming from behind him and he as good as jumped out of his skin as a skateboard narrowly missed hitting him. Its rider niftily scooted around him and then promptly came to a standstill.

'Hi, Felix,' said Ivy, taking off her helmet.

'Oh, I was just coming to see you. Did you...?'

'Yes, we've heard. Past records. Hissy fits. The palace! You see what I mean about that place. It's really bad.'

'Yes, everyone's in a trance there. No one, apart from me, seemed to be worried about what was happening to them.'

'Yes, if you disrupt the calm, he can't cope. That's how you get out. But you have to do that before he casts his spell on you,' said Ivy.

'Or puts you in the cells,' he added.

'Yes, people get locked up for weeks.'

'Well, hours. Anyway, we have to do something about the place.'

Ivy did not respond but just stared into his eyes.

'Do you fancy a bobolate?' she said after a few moments.

'Oh, yes please.'

'Come in then.'

Ivy went through to the kitchen, and Felix went to join Jo, who was snuggled up next to the log fire, which was crackling away as always.

'Hi, man. Take a pew. How ya doin'?'

'OK. Although not really.'

'What's the problem, man?'

Felix told him all about how he thought Jermaine was being seriously brainwashed and asked him if he could get him back to TWAWKI. But apparently, it wasn't as easy as all that. There were certain procedures that you had to go through first, like getting your haircut, for instance. You had to be returned in the same condition that you were collected in. That's why they took photographs of you on the first day.

You might have grown a bit. There's nothing anyone could do about that, but the haircut's always the big give away. Not that Felix's had changed much since he'd left home.

'So how come you didn't have to chop that lot off?' said Felix, pointing at Jo's long floppy hair.

'Because I grew all this in TWAWKI before I came back. It was really far out too because my parents thought that I was rebelling in the same way as hippies used to. So, I could really feel my previous existence coming through, man.'

'That's really cool.'

'Yeah, it was. Anyway, I'll have a think about Jermaine. We could give it a go.'

'We could,' said Ivy coming in with the bobolates. 'But what good is that going to be for the rest of us on the island?'

'It'll be good for him.'

'Felix, I didn't want to have to tell you this before. But it seems that the time has come. Why do you think that Subaltern's getting away with manipulating those kids in the way that he is?'

'Simple! All the other staff are afraid of him.'

'Do you really think that that is enough to stop a whole body of people, whose job it is to keep the world in balance, from fighting for what they believe to be right.'

'Yeah, man,' interjected Jo. 'They say that their mission is to ensure good wins over evil!'

'Exactly,' said Ivy. 'Anyone who is devoting their life to doing that is not going to be defeated by...Do you know what the word *subaltern* means, by the way?'

'No.'

'It means second-in-command. And that's all he is. He's a little man who thinks he's big. No one's really going to be afraid of him. There are far more powerful forces at play here than him. Do you really think that your past lives were so bad that they weren't able to tell you about them this morning?'

'No, I don't.'

'Someone's obviously tampered with your records.'

'Yeah, that's what I thought and that's what my guide felt as well.'

'Well, she was right. There is a large and terrifying network of evil here on this island and we can either walk away from it or find out who's behind it and then take them on ourselves.'

'Is that what you're trying to do?'

'Too right it is. Don't forget. It's not just here that's going to suffer, but the whole of TWAWKI. This network of evil is trying to infiltrate the minds of Springers and corrupt them. Jo feels the same.'

'Yeah, man. They tampered with my records too. Only I knew who else I'd been and the head teacher – before he became the Head – verified what I said. So, I was able to keep going to the school. But there's some weird stuff going on there. Not from him, not from Mrs Snapdragon, not from Mr O'Flaherty, but some of the others...Oh, boy!'

'So, what should I do?' asked Felix.

'Go back tomorrow. See what they have to say. You don't have to join our little coven, so to speak, but God help you if you don't.'

'This is all getting too much for me. I don't think that I can handle this anymore. What's going on here? Is Mrs Higgins OK?'

'Yeah, yeah. You'll be fine with her. She's just in her own space, man. Why don't you go back there now and rest, man. It's been a long day.'

'It sure has.'

'Your wolveraffes are waiting!' announced Ivy.

'Do you mean to say they are...guarding me?'

'What else would they be doing? Spying on you?' said Ivy.

'Well, I suppose that wouldn't be much use – unless they could talk.'

'Exactly. They do my bidding and they do it very efficiently.'

'Well, thank you...At least there's something that I can trust on this weird, freaky, mind-boggling island.'

{ 9 }

Sixes and Sevens

Mrs Higgins had done herself proud at the dinner table that night and her Hollow Pie was better than anything that Felix could have expected. It was the way she made her pastry – not too thick, not too crusty, just slightly buttery, so that it melted in the mouth. And as for the vegetables! You could almost taste the technicolour!

For just one moment Felix was lulled into a false sense of security about where he was. If only Hollow Island was as pure and wholesome as Hollow Pie. Maybe it was. Some of the time. But it certainly wasn't right now.

'Mrs Higgins?'

'Yes, dear.'

'You know you said that when Stonehenge is red, there's something funny going on. Well, it wasn't red this morning, but I'm sure it was pink. And what with my records being changed, those guys bullying me and that weirdo atmosphere at the palace, something's definitely up and I want to get to the bottom of it.'

'Oh, no. You don't want to go meddling with things on this island. There are forces much stronger than any human being can handle. Keep well away. You're not in any trouble anymore. Go off and enjoy yourself instead.'

'Oh, yes. Talking of which...,' said Edith. 'George and Sanjay have asked me to give this to you.'

'What is it?'

'A note. They wanted to apologise for their appalling behaviour and wondered if you'd like to play cricket with them tomorrow.'

'Oh, that sounds cool.'

So, the following day Felix headed off to the school's cricket pitch, which was next to the canal opposite the Venetian Palace. The first person he spotted was The Boy, the one he'd seen on his way to the palace – the one who'd pretended not to be watching him. Amongst the others, in this small group of spectators, was Mr Subaltern. And Ivy was there as well. He tried to wave to her, but she seemed to be looking in another direction. Maybe they weren't supposed to let on to other people that they knew each other.

'Felix!' cried out Sanjay from the pavilion. 'I didn't think you'd come.'

'What are you talking about? I like cricket,' he shouted back as he walked towards him.

'What about us though?'

'Oh. I like you too.'

'Sorry about what we did to you.'

'Don't worry. Here's my chance to take my revenge,' said Felix with a twinkle in his eye.

'No, it isn't. You're in my team.'

'Cool.'

'George!' shouted Sanjay.

'Yeah.'

'Bat or bowl?'

'Oh. Bat, please.'

'OK. Let's get started. Who's in first?'

'Me and Jenny.'

'OK. Get your pads on then.'

The two of them got padded and helmeted up whilst Sanjay's team sorted out their positions. Felix had only ever played with a tennis ball at school, but he had watched loads of games in the field next to his grandpa's allotment.

The day was sharp and clear and the atmosphere on the pitch was very concentrated. This was the type of quiet that he really liked, particularly when all you could hear was the hollow sound of the bat hitting the ball. However, George and Jenny were invincible. It seemed impossible to get them out and – even worse – to stop them knocking out sixes, which they continued doing until bobolate-time.

Despite being on the other team, he congratulated the two star players, while they were digging into iced buns and bobolate, in the pavilion.

'You weren't a pro in your previous whatsit, were you?'

'A professional what?' asked George.

'Cricketer?'

'No, I was an artist as a matter of fact.'

'What, like Picasso?'

'Not as famous as him. But then women weren't, were they?'

'Were you a woman?' said Felix.

'Yeah. I prefer being a bloke though, but hardly anyone here has been the same sex throughout all their lives. A few of the third years have become gender fluid in this life because of that.'

'How do you mean?'

'Well, the reason that we're here on Hollow Island is to help us get in touch with our previous lives – male and female. So, we've all got a bit of both in us. Anyway, let's get this game finished.'

When they went back out, most of the spectators were still there, including The Boy! This time Felix stared over at him, but he looked away. Could this be his mum? Just as he went over to speak to him though, Sanjay called out:

'Felix, get padded up now. You and I are in first. The other side have decided to retire at 250.'

Felix was too distracted to score anything very much. He

kept wondering whether The Boy was his mum and wishing that Jermaine was batting with him. But he wasn't. He was still under the spell of Mr Subaltern. These thoughts were not helping his concentration and at one point he made a real schoolboy error and got both himself and Sanjay run out.

'Well, mission accomplished,' said Sanjay, as they picked up their stuff to go.

'What do you mean?' said Felix, looking round to see if the person who might possibly be his mum was still there.

'You got me back.'

'What was that?' said Felix, realising that The Boy had gone. 'Oh, yes... I suppose I did. Sorry.'

'No, I'm the one who's sorry. I don't know what came over me the other day.'

'No...' said Felix, but he was interrupted by Mr Subaltern.

'Well done, Felix,' he said.

'Well done? But I was out!'

'That's exactly what I mean. You were out, but you didn't...'

'Get angry, sir.'

'You're learning, Felix. Well done!'

'Thank you, sir. What's the best way to get back from here?' he said very quickly as though it was all one sentence.

'Well, if you want the scenic route, climb over the gate in the corner of the field and that'll take you onto The Dragon's Back. Just keep following the path after that. Otherwise...'

'No, I'll go that way. Thank you, sir,' he said, peering over his shoulder towards Ivy, who took a quick look in his direction and made a face at him.

The Dragon's back was exactly as it had sounded. It felt

as though he was creeping along the length of a sleeping monster's spine, with the sides of its chest sloping down either side of him. To his right, there was a perfect view of all the island's landmarks – including a bright red Stonehenge – and to his left, he could see outlines of distant islands, which looked like they were floating just above the sea's horizon.

As he walked, he thought about how much he liked George and Sanjay now and how they had almost become friends. So, what was it that had been controlling them when they were bullying him? Was Subaltern behind it all? Every time he saw the man, it gave him the creeps. Maybe he had done it to provoke him into an outburst of anger so that he could get him into the palace. But why would he have wanted Felix there when he was just the sort of person that he couldn't handle? Nice, calm people like Jermaine, seemed to be far more suitable recruits.

There had to be someone else involved in all of this. Quite possibly there was a whole network, as Ivy had said. He would need to try and find out at school the next day now that he was back in the fold again.

Just as he was thinking this, the ground beneath his feet began to vibrate. It was like being on one of those machines at the gym. He could hardly move, and he had to stand still for fear of being thrown off the hilltop. It was difficult to know what to do next. He needed to get home as quickly as possible. So, every time the rumbling stopped, he would run as fast as he could before the whole thing started up again.

A twenty-minute stroll was turning into a marathon and if the tremors weren't enough, the wind whipped up so furiously that he found it impossible to stand upright anymore. The only thing he could do was to lie on the ground and crawl as far as he could.

All this freaky stuff was then added to by a downpour of what looked like spherical ice cubes, which pelted every part of him. It was like being endlessly slapped across the face. Not only did it hurt, but his muscles no longer seemed to work, and he stopped being able to crawl as his body seized up with the cold and the pain. This must have been what it was like for his former self on that famous expedition – he thought, and for a moment he had a flashback of climbing to the top of Everest. Tenzing and he – Edmund Hillary – were being pounded by lumps of snow, which were dropping off the precipice. Under any other circumstances, no one in their right mind would have continued any further. But with the summit so close that you could almost touch it, they had to keep going. And so did he, Felix Featherstone. Despite the cold, the seizure of his muscles and the shaking of the ground below him, he found a new energy and soldiered on until – that is – he passed out.

{ 10 }

Infection

When he came to, he was still frozen, still wet, but the snow had melted, and Hollow Island was calm again. He picked himself up off the ground, scratched, bruised and sore and got himself back to Mrs Higgins'.

No one seemed to be in on his return and the first thing that he did was to run himself a hot bath so that he could warm up, but his cuts and grazes stung so much when he got into the tub that he had to just dab himself with water instead. He made himself a snack and some hot bobolate, went to his room and picked up *The History of Hollow Island* to see if there was any mention of freak weather on the island. There wasn't, but it did say that because Tritan wasn't tilted like TWAWKI (The World As We Knew It), the climate remained almost the same throughout the year. A bit like spring in the UK. Not today, it wasn't!

There was no doubt that something was out to get him and what he'd been through so far might just be the beginning. Was it Mr Subaltern? He was the one who had told him to walk across The Dragon's Back. As he lay in bed that night, every creak, every rustle, every sound made him sit bolt upright and listen.

'You had us all worried last night, I can tell you,' said Mrs Higgins, as he came downstairs the following morning. 'We were wondering what on earth had happened to you when you still hadn't appeared by 7.00pm. An hour after curfew. You must have finished the cricket match by then. But then Edith suddenly thought that you might have gone to your room before we all got back. She's very wise, that girl. And sure enough, there you were...out for the count.'

'Was I?' he said. Maybe he **had** slept for some of the night then.

'Sorry, Mrs Higgins. I was just so cold after that storm.'

'Which storm?'

'The snowstorm and all the rumbling.'

'When was that?'

'Yesterday afternoon.'

'Oh. I was out getting provisions. We didn't have anything like that where I was. It must have been very localised.'

'Yes, it must have been, mustn't it,' said Felix, looking at the grazes on his arms. 'Oh, by the way, Mrs Higgins, who pays for all our food and stuff?'

'Oh, we don't have money here.'

'What about credit cards?'

'No, no. We don't have the technology. Nothing modern anyway. Electricity generators and telephones are about as advanced as it gets here.'

'How do people buy stuff then, if there isn't any money?'

'They don't. Money doesn't make this world go round.'

'Oh. What do they do then?'

'People just get given things. Everyone on this island has a role. Either they teach at the school or they're a pupil there or else they're a landlady, a nurse, a printer, a farmer, or a fisherman...'

'But how do they survive without money?'

'How do you survive **with** money? You can't use it here. Everyone gets given clothes, food, and accommodation. What would you want money for?'

'I don't know. Skateboards?'

'Oh, no. They don't allow any of that sort of nonsense.'

'Well, how come Ivy and Jo have got about four?'

'That's what we all want to know,' said Edith as she joined them in the kitchen. 'Ivy gets special privileges.'

'You don't like her, do you?' said Felix.

'I don't trust her, that's for sure. How come she's got her own house?'

'Got her own house?' exclaimed Mrs Higgins.

'Yes, she's got that cottage all to herself,' said Felix. 'The one on the other side of the bay.'

'That's Mrs Harrington's cottage,' said Mrs Higgins. 'Don't go believing any of that nonsense. She's probably just been out every time you've been round.'

'Oh!'

'And she's got that fake accent,' said Edith.

'What do you mean?'

'Well, for starters, she's not American. She might have been in a previous life, but not in this one. It's just that her parents are British, and she wants to disassociate herself from them. Anyway, she could get away with murder...if she was so inclined.'

'Has there ever been a murder here, Mrs Higgins?' said Felix, wanting to put a stop to this bit of 'Ivy bashing'.

'There's been all number of mysterious occurrences since I've been here. You're quite safe though as long as you stick to the straight and narrow. Anyway, you best get going, you two, or you'll be late for school.'

As they made their way up the tree tunnel to school, Felix was lost in thought. He didn't want to bring up the subject of Ivy again with Edith, but what she'd said was bugging him. Might she not be the person he thought she was?

'Alright, Felix?' asked Edith.

'Yeah, fine,' he said.

But it wasn't. Quite apart from Ivy, he was wondering what was in store for him on his return to school. With people provoking him on one day, his records being tampered with on another and freak weather last night, what was he going to be faced with next? And, more importantly, who was behind it all? It was now his mission to find out.

When he went into Assembly, he looked around to see if The Boy was there. But no. No sign of him.

'Good morning, Springers,' called out the head teacher. 'Today, we should have been having Assembly in the big hall because, of course, today is officially the first day of term. However, we have decided to delay the collection of the second and third years, which is good news for you as it means you will receive more attention than you would normally have done in the second week. Right, if you would form an orderly line, you will follow Mrs Snapdragon as per usual.'

As Felix entered the Warrior classroom, Mr O'Flaherty welcomed him with open arms.

'Ah, Felix. Delighted to see you.'

'Thank you, sir.'

'Now, you won't be able to draw on all your previous lives because there is still some doubt as to what they were, but just as an experiment, I'd like you to stand in the centre.'

Felix did as he was asked. Here was his opportunity to prove that his records had been tampered with.

'Now, we all know so well, from the first day in this room, who you were in your last life. But no one here, including yourself, knows who you were before Sir Edmund Hillary. This is not an exact science. It may not work but just stand still and see if another life comes to you. The one before Sir Edmund Hillary.'

Felix stood completely still.

'Now just allow your thoughts to tell you what time you are living in, the place you are living in, what sort of clothes you would be wearing, what your daily routine is...Is anything coming to you, Felix?'

He shook his head. What if he really had been some monster? How could he give into this exercise? All his life he'd been told that he turned everything to ashes and now he was going to find out why.

'Don't worry, Felix. Just relax.'

'I can't, sir.'

'Alright. Don't relax. Do the opposite. Strike a pose.'

He thrust himself forward and mimed holding a rifle. Did that mean he'd been some kind of terrorist?

'Good. Anyone got any ideas? Sanjay.'

'A soldier.'

Felix nodded and let out a big breath.

'OK. Anything else?'

'A Gurkha.'

'What's a Gurkha, Sanjay? I don't think many people here will know. Or maybe we should ask Felix.'

'A Gurkha is a Nepalese soldier. In World War One, they helped the British out.'

'Absolutely correct, Felix. How did you know that?'

'I didn't, sir. Not before I said it.'

'And what happened to you in World War One?'

'I got shot, sir. Killed in action in 1917.'

'Well that all fits. Edmund was born two years later. Thank you very much, Felix.'

As Mr O'Flaherty had wanted to congratulate him on

the session, Felix was the last to leave the Warriors Room at break time. Wandering along the corridor on his own, he realised that someone **must** have interfered with his records if, that is, his life before Sir Edmund had been as heroic as a Gurkha's was.

Maybe Mr Subaltern had played around with the details of his past lives if he'd wanted him to become part of his palace community. That bit added up, but it couldn't have been him that was responsible for that freak storm. If he wasn't able to manage Felix's anger, there was no way that he could control the weather.

A visit from his multi-coloured dragonfly friend interrupted his thoughts though. Felix looked up to say 'Hello, long time, no see', or at least that's what it felt like after his recent ordeal. It did its usual somersault in response before leading him towards the sanatorium. He wasn't ill or injured, but he thought that he better follow it. As he got to the door though, he stopped and turned to go back the way he had just come from. But the dragonfly caught up with him and dive bombed him several times before returning to the sanitorium door. So, Felix went back and knocked.

'Hello, Felix,' said the matron. 'Don't tell me that you've come down with it as well.'

'What's that, miss?'

'This bug that all the collectors have got.'

'Oh, no,' he said, peering in to see Adrian and nine others flat out on their beds.

'That's a relief. Well, what can I help you with?'

'Oh, I just wanted you to check out the grazes on my arms and legs.'

'You are getting into a lot of scrapes. There's nothing I can do about them, I'm afraid. They should heal of their own accord. Just remember to keep them clean.'

'I will, miss. Thank you.'

What was going on? Most of the collectors, except for Jo, had been struck down with a bug. This was too much of a coincidence. They'd been told that the second years were not coming back when they should have done. This must be the reason. But why had no one just come clean about it?

Felix had to let Jo know about this immediately. So, he rushed down to the cottage as soon as school was over and knocked heavily on the door.

'Can I come in?' he said, as soon as Jo appeared.

'Yeah. Of course, man.'

'Have you seen any of your collector friends recently?'

'Oh, no. I haven't been out much.'

'Well, I have and they're not well.'

'Aren't they?'

'No. They're all in the sanatorium and they've come down with a really serious bug. That's why the second years aren't back.'

'Yeah. Of course.'

'Although, come to think of it, why haven't you brought any?'

'Oh...um...I was told not to bother until next week,' said Jo.

'Oh, so you knew already?'

'Only that, man. I didn't know it was because my colleagues were ill. No!'

'All I can say is that you were right about it being a whole network of people.'

'What, the collectors?'

'No, whatever is causing all these weird things to happen. It can't be Mr Subaltern on his own. He can't control me, let alone the forces of nature. But who is it that he's in league with?'

'I don't know,' said Ivy as she came down the stairs to join them. 'But it's for you to find out. You're at school all day. You can be our spy in the camp. I'm sure that more will be revealed.'

'Perhaps I should go back and ask the collectors themselves.'

'No. That's not a good idea. They won't tell you anyway. They'll be terrified that whoever is responsible will make them even worse. They won't reveal anything. Just keep your eyes open. That's all.'

'Very well,' said Felix, as he walked over to the front door. 'I'll keep you updated. See you.'

Quite possibly, the collectors would be too frightened to reveal who was behind their illness. But Felix wasn't going to let that stop him from finding out a bit more. He needed to have an excuse to return to the sanatorium and went up the tree tunnel, looking out to see if there were any Janus-facers around.

He was in luck. One was wandering straight towards

him. He stopped still, so as not to frighten it away and then let the thing approach him.

'Hello, little fellow,' he said as he gave it a stroke. True to form, it turned over on to its back and he started rubbing its tummy. The animal rolled its head from side to side while Felix's hand quivered in expectation.

'I wouldn't do that if I were you,' called out a voice from further up the tree tunnel. 'They bite.'

'Oh. Hi, Sanjay. Thanks. No, I've been caught out before with these things. But this one seems to be OK.'

'You won't know until it's gone for you.'

'True!'

'Where are you off to, Felix? Curfew's in a few minutes.'

'Just going back to school to get something.'

'Oh. OK. See you tomorrow then.'

The Janus-facer had now disappeared, and Felix hadn't managed to get himself bitten. He needed to injure himself somehow though. He picked up a branch and tried to scratch his arm, but all it did was to make a red mark. So, he kept on walking with his eyes darting all over the place until he got to the school gates. A couple of empty milk bottles gleamed in the moonlight.

He grabbed them both, took them back down the tunnel and smashed them against a tree. He then took one of the shards of glass and ran it down his knee until he'd made a decent cut. As he hurried back to the school though, he realised that he'd probably done too good a job. Blood was pouring all over the place.

He rang the bell and waited for the janitor to appear.

'Sorry to bother you, but I fell over onto some glass in the tree tunnel, on my way back home.'

'What was glass doing in the tree tunnel?' said the janitor, wrinkling his brow.

'I don't know.'

'You better come in. You know where the sanatorium is?'

'Yes. I do.'

'Well, you better be quick. Otherwise, there won't be any of that stuff left in your body.'

'No. You're right. Thank you.'

After knocking on the door of the sanatorium, he looked back to see the janitor mopping up the river of blood that he'd spilt all the way down the corridor.

'Felix, what brings you here at this hour? Not more trouble, I hope?' said the matron. 'Not another bite from a Janus-facer?'

Thankfully, he hadn't allowed that to happen. It would have been far too obvious.

'No, I fell over onto some glass in the tree tunnel.'

'Now, what would broken glass be doing in the tree tunnel?'

'I don't know, miss.'

'Never mind. Let's get you bandaged up. Come in and sit down where you can find a space. We're full to bursting here at the moment. And hold this against your knee,' she said, handing him a wet cloth.

He did as he was asked and then quickly looked to see if he could find Adrian. It was difficult to work out who everyone was, as most of them were buried under their blankets.

There was however a seat next to the bed that he'd seen Adrian on earlier.

'Evening, Felix,' said a voice from underneath the covers.

'How did you know it was me?' he whispered in response.

'Well, if I can't recognise your voice by now, there's something very wrong with me.'

'There is something very wrong with you, isn't there?'

'Yes, there is. It's not good at all.'

'How come it's only the collectors that have got it?'

'That's what we all want to know,' whispered Adrian. 'But I have a pretty good idea who might be behind all of this.'

'Felix Featherstone,' called out the matron.

'Yes, miss.'

'You are not to go near any of my patients,' she said in a voice completely different from her jovial, friendly one. 'Goodness me. We're quite overwhelmed as it is. We can't have any more of you coming down with this horrible virus.'

'Oh, I'm sorry, miss,' said Felix, as he hobbled over to her desk. 'But has anyone else got it or is it just the collectors?'

'It's just the collectors at the moment. Now let's get this sorted out. Good, there doesn't appear to be any glass lodged in your knee. You can't have fallen too hard on it.'

'No, I didn't, miss.'

'Good. I can put a bandage on now then,' she said, after she'd finished washing it down.

'Thank you, miss,' he said, as she dressed the wound.

'Well, that will be all. Off you go!'

'Thank you, miss.'

But there was no answer. She can't have been happy with him.

Although he had gone against their advice, he still felt that he needed to tell Ivy and Jo about what had happened in the sanatorium. So, he went back down to the cottage to see them again.

'Back again already? Don't tell me you've got some news,' said Ivy as she opened the door.

'I have, actually. It may be urgent too, as it could affect Jo.'

'Oh!'

'I know that you didn't think that it was a good idea, but I went to the sanatorium.'

'You must have done something before that,' she said, looking down at the blood on his trousers.

'Yes, I cut myself on some glass.'

'How convenient!' said Ivy in a sing-song sort of way.

'Well, I did it deliberately.'

'I'd never have guessed,' she said. 'So that you had an excuse to see Matron?'

'Yes.'

'And what did she say?'

'Well, it wasn't what she said. It was what my collector said that was...'

'What did he say then?'

'He just said that it was too coincidental that all the collectors had gone down with this whatever-it-is and he thought that he knew who was behind it.'

'Really?'

'Yes.'

'And who might that be?' enquired Ivy.

'I don't know. He didn't have a chance to tell me. Anyway, I thought I better warn Jo. Just in case anyone tries to do something to him.'

'That's most thoughtful, Felix.'

'I better get back. Curfew's been and gone.'

'Look after that leg,' she said, putting her hand gently on the bandage. 'These things can get infected.'

When Felix got back to Mrs Higgins', he didn't want to talk to anyone. So, he sneaked up the stairs to his bedroom. As he sat down on a chair, he suddenly became aware of a sharp tingling sensation in his knee. Maybe Ivy was right. It could have got infected. Or maybe it was Ivy that had made it worse.

{ 11 }

Judgements

The next morning, Felix woke up in agony and couldn't get out of bed.

'Felix,' called Mrs Higgins at eight o'clock. 'Time to get up.'

'I can't get up, Mrs Higgins. My leg looks like an elephant's.'

A few days in bed was all that Mrs H could suggest, which meant that another excuse to drop into the sanatorium was out of the question. When he finally did get better and returned to school though, he made it his mission to go and speak to the matron before doing anything else.

'Come in,' she said, as he knocked on her door.

'Thank you,' said Felix.

'I'm sorry that I couldn't come down to you. I've been rushed off my feet with this bug that all the collectors have gone down with.'

He looked through the office door into the sick room and saw that it was empty.

'But there's no one here. Does that mean that they're all better now?'

'No. Sadly not,' she said as she started to remove his bandage. 'We had to move them to another site to ensure that whatever it is that they've got doesn't spread round the rest of the school.'

'What is it they have got?'

'No one knows. It's a bit of a mystery. They could probably diagnose it in TWAWKI, but we don't have either the knowledge or the equipment that they have there.'

'Oh.'

'Anyway, your leg has gone down to its normal size, and it doesn't look as if it's infected. We'll leave the bandage off for now so that it can breathe.'

'So, what was wrong with it?'

'I don't know. Another little mystery.'

'Matron!'

'Yes, Felix.'

'Do you think that it's a coincidence that the only people who got the bug were collectors?'

'Now, Felix, do you really think that that hadn't crossed my mind?'

'Of course not.'

'The last thing we need here is a scare but, between you and me, there is something very sinister going on.'

'That's the word I keep thinking of.'

'Is it, Felix? Well, keep it to yourself.'

'I will, Matron. Thank you.'

Felix went back down the corridor and into the hall where Assembly was about to begin and looked around for The Boy again. He hadn't got the infection because it was only the collectors that had been struck down by that. So, where was he? If only he knew what his name was.

'Good morning, Springers,' said the head teacher in his customary welcoming manner. 'And we are all still Springers. Unfortunately, the second and third years still can't be with us as we're a bit short of collectors at the moment. They've all gone down with the flu.'

This was not what Matron had said and whatever it was seemed a lot worse than flu. Was this some kind of cover up?

'Be not afeard,' he quickly added. 'They're all on another site now. So, there's no risk of contagion. This does mean though that you will continue to get special attention as all the guides are here exclusively at your service. Now, instead of attaching you to any particular one today, we're going to give you the freedom to choose who you want to have a one-to-one session with. It's a bit of a free for all, but we can't allow chaos. So, what I'm going to ask Mrs Pettifer to do is to call your names out one by one and then it'll be a matter of 'first come, first served'. If you want to see a guide who's already busy, you are very welcome to wait outside their room. In some cases, you will need to form an orderly queue.'

This was perfect. Although he desperately wanted to track Adrian down and find out who he had been talking about, he might be able to do a bit of detective work himself by speaking to some of the staff. As he looked up at the gallery and waited for his name to be called out, he could see that Asha and Mr O'Flaherty had both already attracted big, long queues. But he didn't need to speak to either of them as he'd already had as much out of them as he could for the moment. The best people to talk to would probably be the ones who nobody wanted to see. The unpopular ones in other words.

When his name was called out, Felix walked up the stairs to the gallery and let his instinct take him to whichever door took his fancy.

'Come in,' said a very distinctive voice.

'Thank you,' said Felix, as he saw that its owner was as precise and particular as he sounded.

'Good morning, Felix. My name's Mr Advocate. How's it all been going since you left the palace?'

'Oh. It's good. I've made friends with George and Sanjay, who were the...'

'Yes, I know what you're trying to say. Good, I'm glad to hear it. So, order has been restored in your life, has it?'

'Well, not exactly.'

'Please. Tell me. That's what I'm here for.'

'Well, it's nothing really. Just some strange things...'

'Strange things are not nothing, Felix.'

'No.'

'Well, what are these strange things?'

'I can't really say.'

'Or rather, you mean you don't **want** to say.'

'Yes.'

'Come on, Felix. You can trust me.'

'When I came back from playing cricket the other day, I got caught in a big storm,' he said, looking him firmly in the eye.

'A storm? What kind of storm?'

'I got bombarded with ice pellets.'

'Where was this?'

'On the Dragon's Back.'

'Interesting,' said Mr Advocate. 'Anyone else experience this?'

'I don't think so, sir. No one else went that way. But I just wanted to know whether this was normal.'

'No. It's not normal at all. It is as strange as you have just described it. Anything else?'

'Well, I still don't know why George and Sanjay behaved the way they did.'

'Boys will be boys, Felix. It's universal. That type of behaviour. Anything else?'

'Yes. The collectors. It seems a bit of a ...'

'Coincidence? Not really. They were all staying in the same accommodation, the Old Barn, that's all. The only one that didn't get it was Jo, because he was at the cottage. Anything else?'

'My records have been changed.'

'We don't have any real proof of that yet.'

'Apart from what happened in Mr O'Flaherty's class the other day.'

'Yes, I heard about that. Just because you came up with someone – a Gurkha, wasn't it – it doesn't **prove** anything. In fact, as far as I understand it, someone else suggested it and you agreed.'

'Maybe. But the big thing is that Stonehenge was pink the other day.'

'Yes, that's what Mrs Butcher said.'

'Yes, but that was on another occasion,' said Felix, almost knowing what was coming next.

'Well, whenever it was, her husband said that she was imagining things. Are you sure that you weren't? It could just have been the light from the sol setting.'

'I don't know, sir.'

'No, nor do I. I don't know what to say, Felix. You've presented me with a whole list of things that are going on around you, which could, on the one hand, be deeply sinister...'

'Yes, that's the word I would use.'

'...but on the other, have a perfectly rational explanation.'

'Apart from the...'

'Apart from the storm, which only you were party to. Do you see what I'm driving at? In a court of law, I don't think your jury would be convinced. Sorry, Felix. This is not what you wanted to hear, is it? However, at least you can put your mind at rest. Things are not nearly as **sinister** as you are imagining. In fact, they're probably not sinister at all.'

'Thank you, sir,' he said, as Mr Advocate got up to shake his hand.

'Thank you, Felix. Stop worrying and start enjoying your time here. Hollow Island is a beautiful place.'

He walked out of the room calmly and collectively, ambled down the corridor to the staircase and then, when no one appeared to be looking, took a flying kick at one of the bannisters.

'Felix!' called out Edith, as she was coming out of one of the rooms.

'Oh. Hi, Edith.'

'So, who's been winding you up?'

'Mr Advocate. He didn't believe anything I was telling him.'

'Oh, yes. He likes to present the counter argument.'

'It's so unfair.'

'Remember who else you are in this world. You don't always have to react like Felix.'

'But he's wrong.'

'I'm sure he is, but instead of kicking the banister, why don't you do something useful like proving that you were right. Anyway, it looks like your friend wants you.'

Felix looked up to see the dragonfly, who did his usual somersault before leading him out of the school's doors, through the tree tunnel and in the direction of the canal. But he couldn't see any point in going back to the Venetian

Palace. So, he walked the other way towards Mrs Higgins'. The dragonfly was having none of this though and kept coming back to hover over his head and then start flying off in the other direction. The more he ignored it, the closer it got to his face and the more of a pest it became, flapping its wings right next to his left ear. So, he gave in eventually and did what it wanted him to do. As Edith had said, he needed to remember who else he was in this world and to do something useful. He couldn't climb a mountain. There were no mountains to climb on Hollow Island. But he could climb up the front of the palace and speak to Jermaine. He had to have another go at him before it was too late.

When they got to the canal, Felix stripped down to his underpants, left his clothes in a neat pile by the side of the canal and took the plunge.

This was not as easy as he'd thought though. As he dived in, he could taste the muddiness of the water and feel its silt against his eyes. He swam up to the palace, pulled himself up onto the forecourt and started his climb up the front of the building. All of its gargoyles and protrusions gave him enough things to hold onto or to use as footings.

'Jermaine,' he whispered as he got up to his window.

'Flix. What you doing?'

'You've got to get out of here. There's weird things going on here and you're right in the middle of it.'

'What sort of things?'

'Well, being hypnotised for a start.'

'Flix, I'm telling you; I'm not being hypnotised. I don't want to leave here, not until I've found out who I am...or was.'

'Well, why were you going round talking like a...'

'Talking like a what?'

'Talking in that posh way they used to in all those old World War Two movies?'

Felix wasn't sure whether he could hold on any longer. His hands were losing their grip, but he had to persuade him. He took his right hand off the masonry, that it was clinging to, and flexed it back and forward and then did the same with the other hand.

'I'm not going to lose my best friend,' he said. 'I'm not going to watch him being taken away...'

At that moment, one of his footings broke off and he was no longer able to keep a grip. His only option was to let himself drop and he plummeted into the water with a huge splash. It was bad enough trying to swim in this murky water but dropping down below the surface was like falling into a black hole. As he came up for air, the front door opened, and Mr Subaltern put his head round it to see what was going on. So, Felix submerged himself underwater. He'd done this at school. His record was 95 seconds. Unable to hold on for any longer though, he came back up again. Mr Subaltern was still there and looked over towards him. He snatched a quick breath and went straight back down again. When he re-emerged the next time, he could see that Mr Subaltern was looking in the other direction. The dragonfly was distracting him – perhaps too much though, as he was attempting to swat it with his copy of Hollow Times. He picked up a stone from the bank of the canal and flung it as far as he could to distract him and then went under the water again. This was killing him. He couldn't do any more of these. Fortunately – as he came up for air again – he heard Jermaine's voice, calling out from his window.

'Excuse me, sir.'

'Yes, Jermaine.'

'I think I'm ready.'

'Oh. Jolly good. Let's go into my office.'

As soon as they were inside, Felix swam up to the palace and climbed up through one of the arches.

'So, you think you're ready to talk?' he heard Mr Subaltern say, just as he'd positioned himself under the office window.

'Yes, sir,' answered Jermaine.

'Very well. Have you rehearsed what you are going to say?'

'No, but all I do know is that I'm prepared to say whatever comes into my head. I'm no longer afraid of the truth.'

'Off you go then.'

'I am in a Second World War plane. A Spitfire. Flying high above the clouds.'

Jermaine's voice suddenly became like the posh one he used when he was mucking around. Only this time, he wasn't joking. He was for real.

'It feels like another world and my best friends are up here too, flying in formation either side of me. There is no one down below on Earth who could possibly be a better friend. No one else understands how exhilarating it is, after sitting around playing chess for ten hours and then suddenly getting the call for you to scramble...to run as fast as you can towards your plane and take it up into the air in seconds.

We suddenly find ourselves head on with an oncoming fleet of Messerschmitts. We exchange fire, but five of my chaps are hit and twirl down through the clouds...and into the sea. I knock down as many of the other side as possible and then fly back to base – a sole survivor. No one else understands how it feels to be in a plane on your own – a sitting target. And no one else understands what it is like to lose your best friend when you are in this other world.'

Felix felt a shiver down his spine.

'Carry on,' said Mr Subaltern.

'Back on the ground, the dispersal hut is empty, but it's crowded with ghosts. I may have been lucky to have survived, but at that moment I wish so desperately that I hadn't. How can I still have life when my best friends haven't? What right do I have to still be here?... Can we change the subject, please?'

'We will indeed. Well done, Jermaine. You've got there. You've done it.'

'Thank you, sir.'

'You will go back to Mrs Higgins tomorrow a new man.'

That was all Felix needed to hear. So, he dived back into the canal and swam as far as he could underwater without opening his eyes, nostrils, or lips. The narrowness and straightness of the channel ahead were the only thing which gave him confidence that he was heading in the right direction. As he emerged, he continued swimming as fast as possible to the end. He then climbed out of the water, looking like a weird creature emerging from a lagoon, covered in mud and vegetation. He quickly got dressed and was just about to run back along the cliff path when the dragonfly appeared in front of him. A series of semi-circular movements followed in quick succession.

'You want me to turn round?'

His friend did one of his somersaults.

Looking back behind him, there was The Boy – watching him from a distance. Finally, here was his opportunity. But, as soon as Felix started walking towards him, The Boy ran off in the other direction. Felix chased after him as quickly as he could, but the mud and slime that were caked all over his body were slowing him down.

'Hey, wait!' shouted Felix.

But The Boy just gave a sideways glance and disappeared into some woodland. Felix followed but couldn't see where he'd got to. So, he stopped still and listened. But there was only silence. He must have been hiding.

'Hello,' called out Felix. 'Hey, don't be scared. I just want to talk to you.'

Again, there was nothing.

So, he pretended that he was giving up and went back out of the woods. Once he'd got onto the cliff path though, he found a bush to hide behind and sat there motionless. When The Boy finally appeared, Felix sprang out. But this just sent him running again. And when the dragonfly circled around Felix's head, and then darted along the cliff in a homewards direction, Felix got the message. It was time to turn his attention to other matters.

The first thing he needed to do was to pay Ivy and Jo a visit and tell them about his new discovery.

'Hi, man. How y' doin?' said Jo as he opened the door. 'What's going down? Hey, you're all muddy, man.'

'Yeah, I know but it was worth it. I think I might have made a bit of a discovery. Mr Subaltern's not the monster that we thought he was.'

'No?'

'No. Definitely not! He's just helped Jermaine to find his previous self. I heard it all.'

'You've got a few things to learn, young Felix,' Ivy intervened. 'The devil plays devious games and you've just fallen for one.'

'Are you sure?'

'Yes, of course. Some other problem will mysteriously appear for Jermaine and there'll be a new diagnosis, which will mean that he'll never get out. Ever!'

'Really?'

'Yes. I should know. I've been in there myself.'

'But you got out!'

'Yes. Only because I worked out how to play the man at his own game. Believe you me, the man is evil. There's no two ways about it. We just need to work out who else he's working with. Don't be fooled by anyone here.'

'No, I won't.'

'Well, let us know when you have any leads.'

'I will.'

'Oh. And Felix!'

'Yes.'

'Take this,' she said, handing him a bracelet with an emerald stone on it.

'What is it?'

'It's for good luck. You need it right now.'

'OK,' he said, tucking it away into his pocket.

On his way back home, he fished out this curious curio. The stone shone strangely in the moonlight. It did not feel that lucky though – just a bit unsettling.

{ 12 }

Possession

The next morning, Warriors class was taken to the Exhibition Room, where Mr O'Flaherty had laid out a whole range of artefacts that had some relevance to their past lives. This included a length of rope that was used on the Everest expedition and a pair of Martin Luther King's spectacles. Felix's eyes lit up as he looked at them all individually. It reminded him that he had, in his pocket, his own personal ornament, which he slipped onto his wrist.

'Now today, we have a little treat in store. Something to stimulate the mind, the spirit, not to mention the soul. I'm going to let you have a wander and have a look at all these precious items before we discuss their relevance. You are all, of course, very trustworthy but I will impress upon you that not only are they precious, but we have gone to great lengths to obtain these items since we discovered who you all were. Some of our collectors made special trips back to TWAWKI – before they got ill, that is – to secure them. All righty. Off you go, Ladies and Gentlemen!'

Felix picked up a huge wide-brimmed hat with artificial flowers attached to it, took a quick look at it, and put it down again. He then moved on to a 1940s telephone, made from Bakelite plastic, and picked up its receiver.

'Mayfair 142,' he said in his silly posh accent. 'Who do you wish to...?' He continued until he felt something being put onto his head.

'Suits you,' said Sanjay as he turned round to see who had done that.

Felix took the hat off, saw that it was the floral one and threw it across the room to Sanjay, shouting:

'Not as much as it would you. Put it on!'

'OK,' said Sanjay.

He then picked up a sequin dress and threw that over to Sanjay.

'And why not try this one on for size while you're at it!' he called back.

Sanjay picked it up and held it up to himself. Everyone laughed.

'Oh. So, you think that's funny, do you? How about this then?'

Felix went up to the table, picked up one end of it and allowed glass bowls, delicate wooden boxes, and everything else to go crashing onto the floor and break into little pieces.

The whole room went silent, and Mr O'Flaherty intervened.

'Felix Featherstone! Are you aware of what you have just done?'

'Yes, I've just knocked over a table at a jumble sale. So what?'

'As I said at the beginning of the lesson, these items...'

'...are complete and utter garbage,' Felix cut in.

'I think that we've perhaps gone a bit too far, Felix. Have you forgotten what noble people you were in your past lives?'

'Do you really think that I believe in all that RUBBISH?'

'Come here, Felix.'

'No, you come here!' he shouted. A small part of him was looking down on himself in amazement that he could be so rude. He'd never gone this far before. But the rest of him was so filled with rage and anger that this outburst was impossible to control.

'I'm warning you, Felix.'

'And I'm warning you. Don't mess with me. I'm in a bad mood today.'

'All right,' said Mr O'Flaherty. 'We won't mess with you,

but you will be taking yourself to see the head teacher right now. You can explain to him...'

'I'm not taking myself.'

'Very well. In that case, **we** will take you.'

'Who's we?'

'Me – for a start,' replied Mr O'Flaherty, who was now showing a side of himself that none of his pupils had ever seen before.

'Come on then. Try it. You see if you can take me.'

'Grab him, Warriors,' cried out Mr O'Flaherty and a couple of the bravest boys got hold of either arm. This was not enough though. Felix threw them off in seconds.

'And again!' shouted Mr O'Flaherty. This time three boys and three girls got hold of him. He was now kicking and screaming. Four of them had a limb each whilst the other two held onto his torso. They marched him down the corridor to the head's office.

'Don't worry about that. We'll go straight to the Venetian Palace.'

Not for one second did Felix give up the struggle as the group carried him down through the tree tunnel, along the cliff path and up to the canal.

The ferryman used some of his rope to restrain him before putting him into the gondola. The journey down the canal was even slower than usual and Felix lay on the floor of the boat, kicking against the sides of it.

Mr O'Flaherty's helpers carried him through the front door of the palace and over the Bridge of Sighs, which should on this occasion have been renamed the Bridge of Screams.

When they took him down to the ancient old cells on the ground floor, Mr O'Flaherty handcuffed him to a chain on the wall and removed his lucky charm.

'Let's leave him to cool off,' said Mr O'Flaherty as he ushered the pupils out and shut the door behind him.

A shaft of light, which beamed through the cell's tiny window, was only just strong enough for Felix to be able to make out the jagged stone walls and uneven concrete floor, which was both damp and smelly. He found himself just dropping down onto it though, as he wondered how he was going to stop having these tantrums once and for all.

There was a flapping noise coming from the corner of the cell. A tiny bird, a fledgling, was trying to get itself up off the floor. Once it was on its feet, it attempted to fly into the air. But each time it did so, it would end up falling onto the hard concrete and hurting itself. This did not stop it from keeping on trying, however. Felix counted its number of attempts until eventually, on the eighth, it was finally properly in flight and swooping around the cell with great delight. It headed towards the window and perched itself in between a couple of bars. As there was no glass, it was able from there to head off into the open sky. Felix just watched as this little creature found its freedom.

Why had he got so angry? About a stupid hat. He'd turned over tables before, but then shocked himself into stopping. He'd never taken on a teacher. And he really liked Mr O'Flaherty. What would have made him behave like that to him? Unless it was something to do with that 'lucky charm'. That's what George and Sanjay were wearing when they were being so horrible to him. Maybe the emerald stone had made them behave like that.

He became aware that there was someone in the room with him. Only he couldn't see them. He just felt their presence. A voice – just like the one that he had had when he was Edmund Hillary – spoke to him.

'The best conquests are the ones where you defeat things that are wrong in yourself or in others.'

This was interrupted though by a key turning in the door. It was Mr Subaltern.

'So, Felix,' he said in his high-pitched voice. 'You've had a bit of a time, I hear.'

'Yes.'

'Now, I'm going to detach your handcuffs from the chain, so that you will be free to walk around the room,' he said. 'But the door is locked from the outside, so you won't be able to get out.'

'Oh,' muttered Felix, as the guide released him from his chains. He got up and stood completely still, staring at the floor.

'Look at me, Felix,' continued Mr Subaltern. 'You're not a bad kid, but you do – as we both know – still have a severe problem with your anger issues.'

'Yes, sir.'

'Why do you think this is?'

'I don't know, but people...'

'Therapists?'

'Yes, therapists think that it's something to do with my mother dying on my second birthday, sir.'

'Why does that make you angry, Felix?'

'I always thought that it was just so unfair, but now I know that it was my fault.'

Mr Subaltern looked into his eyes and changed his tone completely.

'Why was it your fault?' he said.

'I don't know. But my dad seems to think it was. If I hadn't been born, she wouldn't have died.'

'No, no. That is not your fault, Felix.'

Felix couldn't answer.

'Now, Felix. I'd love to say that we could let you back into the palace itself. However, we are not able to take that risk. I'm sorry to say that you are still a liability. If you flipped again, you could do some damage. But I will get the staff here to provide you with whatever food that you desire.'

'Thank you, sir.'

'I can see that you are no longer showing signs of volatility. So, I think perhaps that we can allow you to have some visitors. There will be **someone** outside the door however, just in case anything should happen. Do you understand?'

'Yes, sir.'

'Jermaine, you may come in,' he called out.

The door was unlocked, and Jermaine came straight over to Felix and put his hands on his shoulders.

'I'll leave you to it then,' said Mr Subaltern as he went out, closing the door behind him.

'Where's your wristband?' he said.

'Oh, um. Mr O'Flaherty took it off me when he put these on,' he said, pointing to the handcuffs.

'Are you OK now?' said Jermaine.

'I don't know. I don't really understand what's going on,' replied Felix.

'I do. It's all down to the wristband, or rather the emerald stone that's mounted on it. It was the same with George and Sanjay when they wound you up the other day. When they saw you were wearing one during your explosion this morning, they put two and two together and realised that that was what had set them off.'

'But what can an emerald stone do? Does it have some kind of power?'

'Yeah, it exaggerates your emotions times ten. Maybe some sort of force takes you over. Sanjay and George both admitted they had teased people before, but they'd never bullied them like they did with you. You often get angry but not like you were this morning. Ivy gave one to me too, but I didn't wear mine.'

'So why is she giving them out?'

'She isn't anymore. She'd found a box of them marked 'Lucky Charms' in her cottage. But now she knows they're not, she's taken them to the school and asked them to deal with them.'

'So, does the school understand what happened to me?'

'I don't think that they want to admit that these things are that powerful. They don't want to stir up a scare. And they know that you get angry. But I know that when you lose it, you just let off a bit of smoke. This morning, it wasn't smoke though. It was a full-on New Year's Eve firework display. You were consumed by another power.'

'Yes.'

'Anyway, you've got another visitor. I will leave you to it.'

He opened the door to let himself out and to let The Boy in.

'Hello, Felix. I'm Christopher.'

'Hi, Christopher. I've seen you around,' said Felix, looking him in the eye.

'Yes, yes. You have,' said Christopher. 'I'm sorry that I kept running away. I wanted to wait until I'd got to know my former self a bit better before I spoke to you, because...I am...I was your...'

'...my mother?'

'Yes, Felix. Judy Featherstone.'

Felix nodded.

'Yes, I was and – now I know that – I find it difficult not to keep looking at you and making sure that you're OK.'

'How long have you known?'

'I found out on the first day and I've spent the last few days reminding myself of that life. That's why I haven't been at school because I needed to spend some time as Judy Featherstone before I met you. And I want you to know that I'm incredibly happy to meet you. I also want to tell you that I'm really happy in my life. Judy Featherstone is now Christopher Williams, and he is – I am – incredibly happy. So, you must stop feeling guilty.'

Felix didn't answer for a while.

'But you shouldn't have died,' he said eventually.

'I know. I wish I hadn't, but I did. I should have been looking where I was going.'

'You had an accident?'

'Yes. A car crash. It was your birthday, and we took you out in the car. But you weren't very happy in the back on your own. So, your dad came to join you and sang 'Happy Birthday' to you. But then his phone went, and it was still in the front. He told me to get it. So, I leant over to pick it up. I should have ignored it, but I didn't. And then...I've only just found this out because I died instantly. You were just unconscious for a few minutes.'

'Oh, I'm so sorry. Did you know that I was a Sagacitor?'

'As far as I can remember – yes, I did. I am so sorry.'

'You mustn't be. I just wish that you could have stayed alive, that's all.'

They were interrupted by a knock on the door and in came Jermaine with Mr Subaltern.

'Do you think he's going to have another one of his tantrums now?'

'No, I don't. Take him back to Mrs Higgins'.'

'Thank you,' said Jermaine.

'But Jermaine,' he said, taking off Felix's handcuffs.

'Yes, sir.'

'We still can't allow him back to school – not until the shock of today has died down and we can be more certain about his records. In the meantime, Felix, you better get yourself up to the bathroom and we'll get you a change of clothes. It stinks in here.'

{ 13 }

Home Truths

As it was dark on the way home and the moons were hidden by clouds, it was impossible to see what colour Stonehenge was. That was probably all for the good though as tonight was not a night for more distress. It was a night for celebration. And that's what they got. When they opened the front door of Mrs Higgins', the smell of roast something-or-other wafted through the air.

'Now don't go thinking that I do this every night. But this one is a special one. So, let's sit down and dig into the roast to celebrate.'

'If I'd known this was going to happen, I'd have made a cake as well,' said Edith.

'Do you think that I hadn't thought of that? Well, we haven't got a cake, but we do have Mrs Higgins' Dreamy Pudding, *la specialite de la maison*.'

'What's that in English?' asked Jermaine.

'The speciality of the house. It's legendary right across this island.'

'Hurrah!' they all shouted in unison.

The roast dinner lived up to all Felix's expectations. The vegetables had that deliciously crispy exterior and a tang of wood smoke permeating through them.

'I'd like to propose a toast,' he said, 'to the beginning of a new chapter, here on Hollow Island.' For tonight, at least, they could forget about the dark side of this strange place.

'Yeah, man!' agreed Jermaine. 'We've survived the hard times. Now it's the fun times.'

'Well, we can certainly do that now that we all know who we are – or rather were,' said Felix.

'Yes,' said Jermaine, who then went on to tell them about his revelation and explained that the reason that it had been so difficult to return to his previous self was because that person had been so tormented for most of his life and had never been able to get over the loss of so many of his friends. He'd also suffered from survivor's guilt and found it difficult to continue going on living when so many of his best friends were dead.

'So how come you've never had a problem flying fighter jets around the park then?' asked Felix.

'Flying fighter jets round the park?' exclaimed Mrs Higgins. 'Well, I ask you. What do they let youngsters get up to on TWAWKI these days?'

'Oh, no. It was only pretending, Mrs Higgins.'

'I suppose I was sort of enjoying the thrill of it all...'

'...without realising its significance,' said Edith finishing his sentence.

'And it's only now that you know the full story,' concluded Felix.

'Yes, I guess I won't want to be doing that for a while.'

'No, you won't,' said Mrs Higgins. 'Dreamy Pudding, anyone?'

'Yes, please,' they all responded in unison.

'Felix?' said Edith, as Mrs Higgins was serving up.

'Yes, Edith.'

'I quite fancy meeting your friend, Ivy.'

'Do you?' said Felix. 'Actually, I'm not sure that she is a friend. After all the trouble she's caused me. First of all, giving Sanjay and George the bracelets – and then me. That's not what I call a friend, even if she didn't know what she was doing.'

'Well, maybe she did,' said Mrs Higgins as she gave Felix a bowl of Dreamy Pudding. 'I've never trusted her ever since she said that Mrs Harrington's cottage was hers. We need to get to the bottom of that. I haven't seen Deidre for a while.

She's not one to go out very often, but I usually see her at the fruit and veg market on Tuesday.'

'What should we do then?' said Edith.

'Well, if you really want to see Ivy, why don't you try and get her to tell us what's really going on?'

'Easier said than done.'

'Not if you play her at her own game and pretend that you want to get a house of your own,' said Mrs Higgins.

'Yes. Good idea,' said Edith.

'Then you could ask her if she's got any more of those wristbands left,' said Felix. 'Although she might report you for being a troublemaker.'

'Oh, no. I don't think she will. OK. I might do that then.'

Having had the day he'd just had and Dreamy Pudding on top of it, Felix was beginning to feel sleepy. So, he went up to his room, lay down on his bed and began to doze off. He was suddenly awoken however by a visit from his friend – the dragonfly.

'What is this?' he blurted out as he came to. 'Oh, it's you. Hello. You don't want me to go somewhere, do you?'

The dragonfly did one of his somersaults.

'Now?' exclaimed Felix.

It did a repeat.

'Are you quite sure? I'm knackered.'

It went into a continuous rolling somersault.

'OK,' said Felix wearily and got up out of bed.

'I suppose I need to get dressed now, do I?'

The somersault just kept on going.

When he was ready, his friend – as always – led the way.

Felix crept down the stairs and out of the front door. After a few minutes of walking though, he came to a sudden stop.

'Hang on,' he said, when he'd worked out that it was leading him to Ivy and Jo's. 'I really don't want to go down there at the moment.'

This sent his multi-coloured friend into a frenzy. He repeated the same action over and over again – flying forward a few feet and then coming back to get him, until eventually he gave in.

As they reached the house, instead of leading him to the front door, the dragonfly behaved in the same way as he had at the Venetian Palace. Felix understood what to do and crouched down underneath one of the windows. He could hear Ivy talking to someone.

'Oh, yes. So, you're the one that's sharing a house with Felix and Jermaine.'

Had Edith gone down there already?

'Yes. And I was beginning to feel a bit left out as they've hung out with you, and I haven't.'

'Why, is this supposed to be a cool place or something?' said Ivy.

'Yes, of course. You're the only pupil who seems to have their own house. It's amazing!'

'It really is, isn't it!'

'You know, I might be totally wrong about this, but I feel that you could be someone who thinks a bit like I do. A sort of kindred spirit.'

'Really?'

'Yeah, I do. And I wanted to talk to you about that.'

'What's there to talk about exactly?' said Ivy.

'Let's put it this way. I've only been here a few days, but I don't think that I could stay here any longer without...how shall I say it?... changing a few things.'

'What? The way the school is run. Things like that?'

'No, no. Much more than that. Now, you may want to report me for this, but I'm going to take the risk anyway.'

'What do you mean?' said Ivy.

'I don't know about you, but I had some really dud past lives and my current one, back in TWAWKI, isn't much better.'

'Right,' said Ivy.

'In fact, I really hate my life in TWAWKI. So, things have got to change, and I think that this is the place where I can make that happen.'

'Too right. That's exactly how I felt too. I was such a good person in all my previous lives, but I was treated so badly in some of them, just like I have been in this one. In my last one, I had a horrible time. I was tortured in a prisoner-of-war camp. And in one of my first ones, I was executed. I was Lady Jane Grey – the good queen who ruled for only nine days. When I discovered that last year, I decided that I was not going to let other people ever get the better of me. In fact, I decided that I was going to become the queen that I never was...So what are you thinking of?'

'Well, for a start – if I could get my own house, like you have.'

'Yeah, that would be good.'

'Now, the fact you've done it means that you must know how to....'

'...work the system?' suggested Ivy.

'Exactly. And it seems that it might not be that hard. There's no police here, the head teacher's not much older than either of us. Who's really in charge?'

'Sure.'

'But that would be just the beginning.'

'The beginning of what?' asked Ivy.

'Taking over this island. That's what.'

Felix's head bumped against the windowsill.

'What was that?' said Ivy.

'Oh, nothing,' said Edith and then continued. 'I'm only saying this to you because you are the only person that I've met so far who would be brave enough and strong enough to do it.'

'Thank you,' said Ivy. 'And what would you do if you took over the island?'

'I'd put an end to school for a start. We could – if you were to join me – use people to work for us, to build a whole little kingdom for ourselves here and have our own palace.'

'What, like the Venetian one?'

'Yes, we could take it over and develop it. And we could call it Pandemonium.'

'Isn't that what the devil called his?'

'Yeah, maybe. Anyway, are you in – or are you out?'

'I'm in. In fact, I've already started paving the way,' said Ivy. 'I want to be Queen Ivy and I want to rule Hollow Island. You can be my second-in-command. We don't need the school or the guides. We just need ordinary people to be our subjects. And we only need a handful of Sagacitors – a few collectors to bring people here. And you and me to control the spirits – a thing that only Sagacitors can do.'

'The spirits?' said Edith.

'Yes, there are various forces that I've already got control of.'

'How have you done that?'

'I found this book – under a loose floorboard in my room. It taught me how to speak to the spirits that inhabit this island. I think that the last person who lived in this cottage was into all that sort of thing. Anyway, they welcomed me with open arms – the spirits, that is.'

'Do they want anything in return?'

'No idea. All I know is that I have harnessed all sorts of natural phenomenon on the island and started to use them for my own benefit.'

'Oh, yes.'

'You've probably witnessed some of my actions. Your friend, Felix, for instance.'

'Oh, yes.'

'I did a couple of things to him.'

'What were they?'

'By making his life here so unpleasant, I thought that he might want to rebel against the system and become part of my splinter group. I thought I might get him on to my side.'

So, it **was** Ivy who had been responsible for all this skulduggery. Why had he been so gullible and fallen for her charms? He zipped over to the front door and was just about to hammer on it, when he realised that if he burst in now, everything that Edith was trying to do would be ruined. So, he took some deep breaths and returned to his original position and listened intently, as Ivy explained how she had gone up and changed his records in the logbook. He then heard her tell Edith about some Sagacitors who had been executed on Hollow Island in Medieval times and whose spirits had remained there ever since. With the assistance of the emerald charms, she had used these lost souls to take possession of George and Sanjay.

'You weren't responsible for Felix's set to with Mr O'Flaherty?' she exclaimed.

'What do you think? Yes, of course. I was just taking advantage of his volatile nature.'

'And what about the collectors in the sanatorium?'

'Well, we don't want any second or third years coming back this year, do we? They'll be on the school's side. It'll be a much harder battle if we have them to contend with as well.'

Although this was Felix's cue to go, one of the wolveraffes had begun to stir. It looked up at him and he gave him a little wave back before stroking it with the tips of his fingers. It didn't growl. Why would it? This thing had accompanied him on several walks, but not tonight. She dropped her head gently on to the ground, shut her eyes and seemed to go back to sleep.

Felix crept away slowly from her, so as not to cause any aggravation, until he'd reached the cliff path. Looking back, he could see that it had now got up, as had the rest of the pack. All he could do was to run. And run he did. All of them were coming after him, but not in the slow, measured way that they had been before. They were racing now.

Although he had a head start on them, they were catching up by the second. The dragonfly, who had obviously got wise to this, led him off the path and into one of those tunnels, like the one he went through to get to school.

Felix ran as fast as he could through it, expecting to see some area of safety ahead of him. That was not to be though. In fact, it seemed to be leading to a dead end. He was running straight towards a rock face whilst these animals, that had turned from guardians to guard dogs, were almost on his heels. All he could do was to grab a branch from one of the trees, turn round and start trying to fend them off. But there were too many of them to prevent any one of them from biting into his arms, legs, or torso.

That was just the beginning though. These things, because they were tall, could go for the neck. Felix watched with his mouth wide open as the leader came straight at him and with his eyes wide open as it hit and bounced off a wall right in front of his nose. The trees either side of him had spread their branches out towards each other and become intertwined. The rest of the pack barked and howled, baring their teeth towards him, but they were unable to touch him. What was this wall of twisted boughs that had miraculously appeared in front of him?

The bewildered pack continued their growling until they had run out of steam. They looked as though they knew they were on a useless mission and when the leader turned away, the rest of them followed. As they got to the end of the tunnel and onto the path, they broke out into a trot and headed back to Ivy's cottage.

As Felix moved forward to peer through them, the branches separated from each other and shrunk back to their original size. For a moment, he stood transfixed. But then he ran. And run. As fast as he could back to **his** cottage.

As soon as he had arrived at Mrs Higgins', he crept in through the front door and was tucked up in bed in no time.

He had barely got to sleep though when he was awoken again. This time it was a knock on the door.

'Sorry, Felix,' whispered Edith through the door. 'I just had to speak to you.'

'Sure,' he said. 'Come in.'

'I've just found out something important, which will affect you in a big way. Your friend Ivy?'

'Yeah. I know,' said Felix.

'How do you know?'

'I overheard your conversation.'

'Did you? How come?'

'Something told me that I should go down to the cottage.'

'Oh. So, you heard what I got out of her?'

'Yes, I did. Boy, that was seriously devious though. The way you went about it.'

'Sometimes, it's the only way.'

'Did you see the wolveraffes?'

'Yes, we heard them from the cottage, howling away. Ivy thought that they were chasing one of those orkins, you know – the things that look like foxes.'

'I was the orkin.'

'Oh, I see. Well as soon as they had returned to the cottage, they accompanied me back here. Anyway, I'd better get some shut eye. And so had you,' she said as she went out of the door.

'So now we know,' said Felix.

'Yes, now we know. The problem is...what do we do about it?'

'I'll tell you what we're going to do about it. Right now, Ivy thinks that she has won. She knows that I'm going to hate everything about this place and be happy to listen to anything that she suggests. I've just been locked up for a start. And she probably thinks that I'm not going to be allowed to go back to school.'

'No, I suppose not.'

'So, I'll be putty in her hands, as long as I don't let her know that I've heard anything from you about her true intentions. So, I'm the perfect person to go and live with her.'

'Go and live with her? But you can't do that. She's evil. Imagine what she might do to you.'

'No more than she's done already. It's my turn to deceive her. I can say that I haven't been allowed back to school or here, or at least that I've been told to find alternative accommodation. Once I'm there, I can find out exactly how she works her powers.'

'I suppose so.'

'It's got to be one of us. We can't just tell the guides. We need to find out much more about her before they get involved. The guides can't go and spy on her.'

'And I wouldn't be able to either. I know too much,' said Edith. 'She's still trying to work out if she can trust me.'

'But she thinks she can me.'

'Yes, she probably does.'

'She sure does. And I'm going,' replied Felix as his head hit the pillow and drifted off into the land of dreams before he could say another word.

{ 14 }

Hypnosis

The next day, Felix came downstairs to find that everyone was out. He helped himself to some breakfast and headed off to Ivy's. As he got close to the cottage, the wolveraffes sat up and looked at him. He stopped still momentarily, but their heads hung low, and their eyes were barely open. So, he went ahead and knocked on the door.

'Hey, Felix. What's going down?' said Ivy, as she opened the door.

'I've been chucked out.'

'Of school. I heard.'

'And home, as well. Mrs Higgins doesn't want me there anymore,' he said, pointing to the bag that he'd slung over his shoulder.

'Great. You're staying with me then.'

'Can I? Thanks.'

'Come on in. I'll take you to your room.'

They went upstairs and she showed him the spare room.

'This feels just like home. It's got the same view as my room at Mrs Higgins' place.'

'Great. Only difference is that here you can say exactly what you want, whenever you wanna say it. But there you probably have to keep your lip buttoned.'

'Yes, and there's **so** many things I want to say.'

'Feel free. It's Liberty Hall here.'

'Do you remember the first time I saw you, I wanted Jo to take Jermaine back to TWAWKI.'

'Yes.'

'Well, I feel the opposite now. I don't want him to take anyone back to TWAWKI. Not Jermaine, not me. I hate every inch of this island – apart from here, of course. So much so that I don't want to leave until I've taken my revenge on it.'

'A lot of people feel like that. Including your friend Edith.'

'Really?'

'Has she not told you about our conversation?'

'No, we fell out. So, we don't talk much now,' he said.

The sound of the front door slamming downstairs put an end to their conversation though.

'Oh, hang on. That's Jo going out. I need to speak to him...Anyway, you're safe here. That's the main thing,' she said as she left him to unpack.

'Yes, I am,' he shouted back to her and then hovered by the doorway, listening intently to what was going on. The front door slammed again, which he thought must mean that Ivy had gone out to speak to Jo. So, he crept down the stairs and crouched beneath the window that he had eaves-dropped through before. Only this time, he was on the other side, of course.

'Ok, so here's the thing, Jo,' he could hear Ivy saying. 'Find out who her friends are and what she's said about me to them – in fact, anything you can.'

'Leave it to me.'

'Awesome. I'll see you this evening. Hopefully you'll have got some leads by then. So, you can report back on your return.'

'What about Felix?' he whispered.

'Don't worry. He's cool. He'll be fine.'

Felix wasn't sure what she meant by that, but he wasn't going to hang around any longer for fear of being caught. So, he crept back up to his room and waited for Ivy to go out.

'I'm off out now, Felix. See you for sups this evening,' Ivy called out from downstairs a few minutes later.

'Thanks, Ivy. You've saved my life.'

'Don't even think about it.'

The front door slammed yet again. Here was his chance to snoop about a bit. Firstly, he needed to find out what had happened to Mrs Harrington. He took a quick peek into the two bedrooms next to his. Nothing particularly strange, except that one of them – probably Ivy's – had a staircase leading up to something above it. He climbed up it as quietly as possible and pushed the squeaky attic door open. The curtains were closed, so it was quite dark, but he could make out a bed with an old lady on it.

'Is that the doctor?' she said.

'Oh, no. I'm afraid not,' said Felix. 'Can I get you anything?'

'Just some water, dear. That's all I need.'

He passed her the glass by her bed.

'Thank you, dear. I think I'll get some more sleep. This virus just won't go away.'

'Are you sure you're going to be OK?'

'Oh, yes. I just need to rest.'

'I'll leave you in peace then,' he said.

There was nothing more that he could do until he'd got some help. So, he went downstairs and looked around.

He scoured the bookshelves but saw nothing extraordinary. Or at least unusual. Some great works of fiction sat side by side with each other, from Charles Dickens to J.R.R. Tolkien, but there was nothing out of the ordinary – at least at first glance. However, when he checked to see which Dickens novels Ivy had got, he noticed that most of them were hard back copies with loose covers.

The jacket for *Great Expectations* looked like it was too big for the book that was inside it though. So, he pulled it out to discover that it had a blank cover and that all its contents inside had been handwritten, not printed. The title on the first page was *Magic and Ritual on Hollow Island.*

He quickly skimmed through the pages. There was a chapter on *Hypnotism* and another one on how to avoid it. That looked interesting. It said that in Rudyard Kipling's *Kim*, the main character prevents someone else from casting their spell on him and making him fall into a trance by going through his ten times table in his head. What else was there? A chapter on *Sleeping Potions* and a picture of the plant, Somnicibus, that you could make one from. It looked like a flowering plant with all its colours reversed. The stem was bright yellow, and the petals were light green.

> *Instructions: Crush up the petals, put into a cup, pour on hot water, and then decant into another drinking vessel through a strainer.*

Just like making a cup of tea with tea leaves. And then there was a chapter on *Calling up the Spirits.* There was a section about the executions that had happened back in the Middle Ages. These four conspirators had been using their new-found powers for their own personal gain and position. It was felt that this was the path that they had set for themselves and that they would continue along it into their next incarnations. The only way to stop them was to kill them on Hollow Island. They would not be able to find an unborn baby to inhabit there. However, what was not anticipated was that their essences would remain – just not in a physical form. Their spirits have therefore inhabited the island ever since.

Next to *Great Expectations* was *A Christmas Carol*. That too had another book inside its jacket. There was a chapter entitled *Calling off the Spirits*. He would have to leave that until another time though. Someone was approaching.

The door opened and in came Jo.

'Hi, man. How ya doin'? You've had a bit of a weird, freaky time out there, apparently.'

'Yeah, I have but I'm safe now.'

'Safe as you can ever be, man. It's really cool here.'

'Is it?' said Felix, looking him straight in the eye.

'Yeah, man. Ivy's so cool and easy going.'

'She doesn't get you to do things for her or anything?' asked Felix.

'What like?'

'Well, I mean, it's her house. So surely, you've got to pay for your keep in some way. You can't do that with money. So, I thought that maybe you'd...or I'd...have to do some chores for her. Her dirty work.'

'Yeah. I do some washing up sometimes, but I really like that. It makes feel at one with myself.'

'No, I didn't mean that. I mean...you know.'

'No, I don't, man,' said Jo.

'Well, for instance, say she didn't like someone, maybe she might get you or I to do something spiteful on her behalf...'

'Oh, no. You've got the wrong idea. She's really laid back. She just wants to help people, that's all.'

'Really?'

'Yes, really! You'll be fine here. Everything's safe here.'

Everything was not safe. Everything was evil. Felix had, of course, been taken in by it all too, but he hadn't been living under the same roof as Ivy. How could Jo possibly say that when he must have seen exactly what she was up to? Felix felt like grabbing him by the collar and 'telling him like it was'. But...**No**, he didn't behave like that anymore.

He couldn't work out whether this guy was either completely oblivious as to what was going on around him or just a very good actor or – and this was more likely – whether he'd been trapped by one of Ivy's spells.

'Do you think that I can take one of these books up to my room?'

'Sure, man. That's what they're there for. Reading! That *Lord of The Rings* is really far out, man.'

'Yeah. I know. I've read it.'

'Yeah. So have I.'

'What, while you've been here?'

'Oh, yeah.'

'What about the Dickens?'

'No, I don't like anything Victorian, man. Not since I spent some time in that classroom.'

'Yeah, I know where you're coming from. I'll stick to the Tolkien then.'

Felix took the book off the shelf and went up to his room.

Several hours later, Ivy came back and called up to him to come down.

'Hi, Felix. We're going to eat in a minute. Jo's cooked some really wicked Trailcon and Haloom thing, haven't you?'

'Yeah, man. You're going to love this.'

'But before we have sups here, we always play a game, don't we, Jo?'

'Yeah, it's great, man.'

'It's just one of those silly things that we've taken to doing. Anyway, I'll start. If you two sit on those chairs and, just to make it all really atmospheric, I'm going to turn the lights off. So, all you can see is the log fire. Now really concentrate and look at that flame. Watch it move. Imagine that you are inside it, flickering away. Keep your eyes on it all the time.'

Her voice became more and more mesmeric. This was exactly what Felix had been expecting. Kim had done his ten times table. He could go one better than that. He tried to remember that algebraic equation that Jermaine had set him that day at school, whilst staring intently at the flame.

'Now, you are losing sense of who you think you are.'

She was almost whispering to them by this point. All the while, Felix was trying to solve $x^2 + 9 = y^2$.

'In fact, you no longer are who you think you are. You've become neutral. You will do as I tell you. Jo, put your hands in the air and say: "I'm an idiot." Five times!'

He did so without any hint of embarrassment.

'Felix, come and kiss my hand.'

This was not difficult. So, he did as she asked.

'Now, put your hand into that bowl of bobolate pudding.'

Again, nothing hard about that.

'And now dig a bit out and smother it all over your face and hair.'

This was disgusting but easy to do. His head just felt sticky and uncomfortable, and he couldn't wait to get into the shower to wash it off. But he would just have to **wait**.

'And now, put your right index finger into the fire, Jo.'

He watched in amazement as Jo followed this instruction. This was dangerous. He'd seen his uncle do this once at a party and he was never able to use his right hand again.

'Don't take it out until I say so.'

He could see that Jo's finger was beginning to scald.

'OK. You may remove it now.'

Jo did so, but without any fuss. He must have been totally under her spell.

'Now, you! Felix.'

Felix placed his finger at the top of the flame and breathed in and out as deeply as possible. This was unbearable. He did still have the equation to work out, of course. Maybe that would distract him from the excruciating pain. If $x^2 + 9 = y^2$ and the unknowns were both positive integers, what were the values of x and y? If x was 2, then x^2 would be 4 and y^2 would be 4 + 9, which equalled 13. No, that wasn't a perfect square. What about if x were 4, then y^2 would be 16. Add 9 equals 25. Now that was a perfect square and y would be the square root of it: 5.

'Alright. Take it out. Get a glass of water for Felix, Jo. His skin's burnt.'

He had passed the test without being hypnotised. So,

Jermaine's equation, which had frustrated him so much at school that day, had turned out to be a life saver.

Although he was in a lot of pain over supper, he was also so relieved not to have fallen for Ivy's powers that the one balanced out the other. Almost! The pie was delicious though. Ivy had not been deceiving him on that score. As they finished up, Ivy let them know her plans for the rest of the evening and the following day.

'After supper, guys, we're going to take the boat to the caves. I have a little mission that needs to be accomplished. Now, from the intel that Jo got on Edith, it looks like she isn't really the person she was making herself out to be the other day. So, we need to get a couple of girls from her class to do some probing. Who are her best friends, Jo?'

'Felix and Jermaine.'

'Girls, stupid!'

'Oh, Jasmin and Jade.'

'Right, does she really trust them?' said Ivy, running her hands through her hair.

'Yes.'

'In that case, we can get them to find out if she was telling the truth or not.'

'How do we do that, Ivy?' asked Jo.

'By getting some of **our** friends to infiltrate their very beings. That's how,' said Ivy, who then turned to look at Felix.

'Are you any good at rowing, Felix?'

'Yes.'

'Well, let's go then.'

{ 15 }

Spirits and Potions

The moons were bright enough for them to scramble down the path to the beach, where Ivy's boat was moored. Once Ivy and Jo were in, Felix rolled his trousers up, pushed the dinghy further out into the water, climbed over the side, sat down, got his oars into position, and started to row.

'Which way?'

'East. Keep going until I tell you.'

'Stop!' she shouted after about ten minutes. 'Now just head into that cave.'

Felix managed to row the dinghy into the sand and then jumped out, catching the rope that Jo had thrown him and securing it to a hook in one of the rocks.

'Take these candles,' said Ivy. 'You've got matches, haven't you?'

'Yeah.'

The inside of the cave was dark and damp, as they often are. Ivy placed the candles in a circle large enough for them to stand in and then went round lighting them. She began to chant as she lit each one.

'Give light unto these poor, forgotten souls. Let them now be remembered and cherished and loved. We come here in peace, only to acknowledge you.'

As she said this, Felix could feel the presence of something standing right next to him. He couldn't see anything, but he could feel that there was someone who was very disturbed standing beside him. Then directly opposite, another one could be felt. This continued until eventually he counted a total of five spirits that had joined them. There was no let-up in that energy as Ivy spoke softly to them.

'I need your help again, my friends. But this is a more subtle task than that of your last assignments. Instead of drawing upon your anger, this time I need you to be devious. Anyone who feels unqualified, I would ask you to step down.'

The energy that had so strongly vibrated opposite Felix was no longer there. He could almost see another two drift away, but the one next to him was as vibrant as ever.

'Good. We have two left. That's all we need. Your 'in-habitees' – the people who you will inhabit – are Jasmin and Jade. I don't have any emerald stones to give them this time. So, you're just going to have to find them by your own devices. Understood!'

There was a movement in the air from both of them.

'Your task is to find out from Edith what her intentions **really** are. Does she want to work with me or is she just deceiving me? In other words, find out what she honestly thinks of me. Tomorrow night, I want you to bring her to the cottage. If she is genuine, we'll all have supper together. If, however, this girl proves to be a traitor – kill her. I don't care how. Push her over the cliff and make it look like an accident. Understood!'

Another shift in the air.

'Good! I am most grateful,' she said, stepping out of the circle and beckoning to Jo and Felix to do the same.

'Boys! Pick up the candles!'

As they returned to the cove, Felix rowed the boat with smoothness and precision. His mind was racing though, trying to work out how he could possibly get a message to Edith. However, there was absolutely nothing that he could think of.

'I expect that you'll both want to get straight to bed,' said Ivy as she opened the front door.

'Oh, yes. Definitely,' answered Jo immediately.

'Yes, definitely,' reiterated Felix.

'Keep vigilant, guys!' she said to her long-necked friends and then locked the door and took away the key.

Felix went straight to his room, rinsed his hair in the basin, dropped onto his bed, and tried to work out a plan. There was no way that he could get out of the house tonight to go and warn Edith. The front door was locked and the wolveraffes were on high alert. If Ivy and Jo were around all the next day, he was stumped unless he could…But overwhelmed by the uselessness of it all, he drifted off into a stupor. A few hours later though, he woke up with a start. Sleep! Of course! He could make up a sleeping potion and give it to Ivy and Jo during the day. He sneaked downstairs, pulled out the book of magic from the shelves and wrote down the recipe and the description of the Somnicibus plant. He put the manual back, disguised in its *Great Expectations* cover, and pulled out *A Christmas Carol.* But a movement from up above made him put it back again and head upstairs to bed before anyone caught him snooping.

The following morning, Ivy played another one of her 'games' with Jo and Felix. So, this was how she kept control over Jo. She'd have to reboot the hypnosis in the morning and the evening to ensure that he never slipped out of it. Another algebraic equation was called for…and quickly…or perhaps he could just return to a dream that he'd once had. The one he had lived for real in another existence – in which the peak of Everest was only a few feet away.

When it was his turn to put his finger in the fire, Felix imagined that his hands were frozen to the bone and that any kind of warmth was welcome even though this was burning him. It didn't matter whether he kept them in the fire or took them out. The pain would be just as bad from the frost bite as it would be from the burning.

'Alright, you can take it out, Felix,' said Ivy.

'Oh, thank you,' said Felix calmly.

Once the ritual was over, he asked Ivy if he could do some gardening.

'It's really just for something to do, apart from anything else. And I quite enjoy getting my hands dirty.'

'Sure. Are you any good?'

'Yeah, I do quite a lot on my grandpa's allotment.'

'Well, I guess I can just leave you to it then.'

He got down to some weeding to begin with, checking with Ivy first that what looked like weeds were weeds and not some precious plants. No sign of the Somnicibus though, at least not to begin with, not until he went down the path to a row of bushes. He took a quick peek over his shoulder to check that neither Ivy nor Jo was looking out of the window, as they had been every so often, and scrambled through the thicket to see what was there: a whole clump of flowering plants, which looked identical to the ones in *Magic and Ritual on Hollow Island* – unmistakable because of their bright yellow stems. He quickly pulled a couple out of the ground and returned to put them into his basket of weeds. Just in time, it would seem, as Ivy came out of the back door.

'Want some hot bobolate, Felix?

'In about half an hour, if that's OK.'

'Sure, I'll hang on until you've finished,' she said as she went back into the house.

There was no sign of either Ivy or Jo leaving the cottage

that day. So, there was no chance of getting away from the place to see Edith or at least to get a message to her. When it got dark, Felix went back into the house. He knew that the girls would be due to make their way down to the cottage shortly, so he had to get on with things.

'That's a great job that you've done out there,' said Ivy. 'I've been meaning to do it myself, but I just can't be bothered. And Jo's useless. He'd pick the flowers and leave all the weeds.'

'Like I nearly did.'

'Do you want that bobolate now?'

'Oh, yes. I'd love one. Do you?' said Felix.

'Yes. I'll make it.'

'No, don't worry. I will.'

'Thanks, Felix. I'm feeling a bit lazy today.'

'Jo!'

'Yes please, Felix.'

He went into the kitchen, pulled the plants out of his pocket, and found a knife to chop the petals up with. He put them into a cup, which he filled with hot water. Once it had all brewed, he poured it through a strainer into a mug and then tipped a bit of his preparation into Ivy's bobolate and some into Jo's. He then hid the rest of it at the back of one of the cupboards in case he needed it later.

'Oh, thanks, Felix. You really are a proper man about the house,' she said as she took the mug away from him. 'Um, Lovely. Nice mug of bobolate, houseboy! What have you put in it?'

'Just the usual stuff,' he said.

'Oh, it tastes a bit different. That's all. It's probably just the way you make it.'

'Yes, probably. Oh, no! I haven't put the garden tools away.'

'Don't worry. You can do that tomorrow...'

'No, I'll do it now if that's all right.'

'I said – you can do it tomorrow,' repeated Ivy.

'Sorry, I just wanted to do the right thing,' said Felix.

'Well, the right thing is to...You know, I suddenly feel a bit tired. And Jasmin and Jade are coming over later, aren't they?'

'Yes, I think they are.'

'Oh, well. I'll probably...'

But with that, she was out for the count.

'Hey, man. What did you put in this bobolate? I'm out of it,' said Jo, as he too slumped back in his armchair and fell asleep.

How long this stuff lasted Felix didn't know, but he had to act quickly. He went out of the front door and walked casually past the wolveraffes, who looked up at him with their dead eyes. His body was shaking nervously, but he managed to keep his cool enough to disguise this.

As he got to the cliff path, the moons were bright enough for him to see Edith walking down towards the cottage with Jasmin and Jade. He should have timed this better. If he ran up to them, he could probably prevent them from carrying out Ivy's orders but that would get the wolveraffes going. He couldn't risk that after what happened last time.

So, he had to continue, for the moment, to just walk slowly towards them.

When an argument broke out between the girls, he knew that this was the beginning of the end. So, there was nothing for it. He had to run up to them. The wolveraffes sussed this from half a mile away and came chasing up towards them. Felix pulled Edith away from the other two and shouted: 'Run!' And run they did.

'We have to get down to the cove,' shouted Felix.

'You grab the boy,' called out Jasmin to Jade, 'and I'll deal with Little Miss Turncoat here.'

'But I'm not a turncoat. I didn't know which side you were on. I thought you both were goody-two-shoes. Anyway, if we don't stop fighting and shift our backsides, those wolveraffes will get us all. The reason why their necks are so long is so that they can bite into our jugulars.'

'What are they?' said Jade.

'These things,' said Edith, pointing to her neck. 'They'll kill you in other words.'

'Let's get down to the beach and into the boat. It's our only hope,' shouted Felix.

The girls ran down the path with the wolveraffes slipping and sliding behind them.

'Jump in! Quickly!' shouted Felix.

As Jasmin, Jade and Edith got themselves seated, Felix shoved the boat out into the sea. The wolveraffes – for some reason – were not entering the water or even getting their paws wet. However, they still were able to reach his legs and were tearing his trousers off him and biting into his flesh, which stopped him from being able to make any progress with his pushing. He was done for and could feel himself getting weaker.

'You've got to get to the cave and...'

But Edith was too busy splashing salt water at the wolveraffes to take any notice. The animals were flinching and shaking, unable to sustain their grip on Felix's legs. They must have hated the stuff and all they could do now was howl.

Felix jumped into the boat, grabbed the oars and started rowing. Despite the pain he was in, the adrenalin in his system gave him the strength to keep going until they had arrived at the cave. He jumped out, tied the boat up and grabbed the candles and matches.

'Come into the cave. I want to show you something,' he said to them.

'Are you kidding?' said Jasmin.

'No. Come in,' he said, arranging and lighting the candles as before. He had no idea what he was doing but he had to do something.

'Please, stand in the circle with me.'

Once they were all positioned, he started to chant.

'Give light unto these poor, forgotten souls. Let them be remembered and cherished and loved. We come here in peace, only to acknowledge you. We are grateful for all you have done for us. It's time to go home now though. Time to go home. Time to go home. Time to go home.'

Jasmin and Jade looked at Edith and him in disbelief.

'Where are we?' said Jade.

'What are we doing here?' said Jasmin.

'Just saying goodbye to some **old** friends,' replied Felix.

'Oh. Can we go back now?'

'Yes, we can,' said Felix.

'Yes, we've done all we need to do in this particular *House for Lost Souls*,' said Edith as they came back out of the cave.

When they got back to the beach, the wolveraffes were still waiting at the water's edge, looking just as vicious as they had done before. Felix rowed the boat up to them and then quickly turned it around and headed back out to sea, round the headland and into the next-door cove.

'Can you swim?' he said to the girls.

'Yes,' they all replied in unison.

'Well, swim back to the beach that we've just come from. I'll distract them in the other cove.'

All three girls jumped out of the boat and did as Felix suggested. In the meantime, he kept rowing the boat towards the next cove. The wolveraffes had by this time climbed up to the top of the cliff and were beginning to come down the path on the other side and head in his direction. Felix pulled the front part of the boat onto the sand and then jumped back in again. The wolveraffes surrounded the boat's bow, but he was sitting right at the other end.

As their barking and howling reached fever pitch, one of the wolveraffes took the lead and jumped into the dinghy. The others followed immediately afterwards. Almost simultaneously, Felix threw himself overboard into the water and pulled the boat out to sea. The wolveraffes were now both terrified and frightened, howling and biting at his hands.

As they got more confident, they stuck their necks out and grabbed the part of his arm that was above the water with their teeth. He used his other hand to splash them until eventually they let go, allowing him to swim round to the front of the boat and grab the rope, which he tied to a rock. 'Good!' he thought. They'd be stuck there until the tide had gone back out and the boat was on dry land again.

Felix swam back round the headland to where Edith was waiting for him. She told him that Jade and Jasmin had gone back home – after they'd received a full explanation – and then helped him hobble up the cliff path.

As they made their way back to the cottage, the wolveraffes' howls became fainter and fainter.

{ 16 }

Return Journey

Felix sneaked in through the front door, hoping that Ivy wouldn't hear him.

'What's that?' she said without opening her eyes.

'Oh, nothing,' said Felix. 'Just wondered whether you wanted another boffee.'

'Oh, yes please, houseboy. I need to wake up.'

He quickly nipped upstairs, washed down the wolveraffes' bites and changed his trousers. Sticking his head out of the window, he signalled to Edith to knock on the door and then ran down to answer it.

'Oh. Hi, Felix. Is Ivy at home?'

'Yes, she's just here.'

'Hi, Ivy. Thanks for inviting me,' said Edith.

'Oh. Hi, Edith,' said Ivy. 'I didn't think that you'd come.'

'Oh, why would that have been?'

'Just didn't. Sorry, I'm really dozy.'

'I'll get your boffee, Ivy,' said Felix. 'Do you want one, Jo?'

'Yeah, man. I could really do with one.'

He went into the kitchen, reached into the cupboard for his potion and made two steaming cups of boffee, one 'with' and one 'without'.

'How's that, Jo?' he said as Jo knocked his one back.

'Yeah, great. Just what I needed.'

'Any better,' said Felix, as Ivy put her cup to her lips.

'Yes, I think I...'

And with that, she was off again.

'Oh,' said Edith. 'Wonder what happened there. You're alright though, aren't you, Jo?'

'Yeah, I'm fine. Much better. Ta.'

'So you should be,' said Felix. 'You didn't have any...'

'Any what, man?'

'Don't worry. Forget about that? Do you fancy playing a game?'

He knew that he had to un-hypnotise him and he had to do it now. But how?

'Hang on,' he said, realising exactly where he could find out. 'That *Great Expectations* book's got a really good one in.'

'I suppose it would with a name like that.'

Felix pulled the book off the shelf and flicked through it until he got to the chapter on hypnosis.

'Here we go. Let's turn off the lights. Now, Jo, look into the fire. The fire is your friend. Think of nothing else and look at nothing else but the flames. They are your friends. At least, you think they are your friends. Let's go and touch them and see if they still are.'

Jo's hands were shaking away as he went and stood by the fire.

'Go on. Touch them.'

He reached out his hand and quickly took it away again.

'I said touch them!'

'I can't.'

'Try!'

'OK. I'll try.'

He put his finger in quickly but withdrew it almost immediately.

'Ow. That hurts.'

'Good.'

'What do you mean...**Good**?'

'I mean...**Good**. Welcome back to the real world, where you can make your own decisions instead of following someone else's orders.'

'You mean...**hers**?' he said, pointing at Ivy, who had got out of her chair.

'Do you think that I am stupid?' she shouted at them as

she chucked the contents of her boffee cup into the air. 'Why on earth would I fall for your lousy tricks twice. I wonder whether my friend Julius is around. Julius!' she called up the staircase.

A door swung shut upstairs and Mrs Harrington's glass of water floated down the stairs.

'Julius. We have two prospective patients here,' she said as she took the glass away from the invisible person. Was this another of her paranormal pals?

'Do your worst!' she proclaimed.

'Run for it, guys,' shouted Jo. 'Go and get help.'

Edith and Felix made a dash for it before Julius could get them. As they got back in through the door of Mrs Higgins' cottage though, everything went blank.

The next thing Felix knew was that he was in his bed. As he tried to get up, his arm didn't seem to want to move. In fact, nothing did apart from his heart which was thumping away, one pumping beat after another. Felix just lay there, looking at the ceiling.

Mrs Higgins came in and talked softly to him for a while. She mopped his brow and disinfected his wolveraffe wounds. This stung, but he couldn't do anything about it.

An hour or so later, Jermaine knocked on the door. Felix couldn't answer, but he came in anyway.

'Oh, Flix. You're awake.'

He couldn't even nod his head. He must have had a worse dose of this virus than the collectors because he couldn't speak either.

'Listen, Flix. I know that you can't speak or move or anything. But can you hear me?'

Felix rolled his eyes around.

'Great.'

It wasn't that great, of course but at least Jermaine could see his eyes.

'Ivy must know that I know what she's up to, but she hasn't managed to do anything about me **yet**. As soon as I saw what had happened to you and Edith, I made myself scarce. When Ivy came looking for me here, Mrs Higgins played the innocent and said that I had gone back to the Venetian Palace for a while. She also asked Ivy if she could do anything about you and Edith, saying that you'd been struck down with that terrible virus. So, expect a visit soon.'

Felix closed his eyelids and opened them again.

'Are you feeling sleepy, Flix?'

He opened his eyes and moved them from side to side.

'No. You're not sleepy.'

He kept his eyes open and thought about how terrified he was of being killed by her.

'You're scared?'

He moved his eyes up and down.

'You're scared because she's not going to cure you. She's going to leave you to die.'

His eyes repeated what they had just done.

'So, I need to find the cure. Do you know where I can do that?'

Felix rolled his eyes wildly.

'Is it in a cupboard?'

He looked at him blankly.

'Is it under a floorboard?'

His eyes didn't move.

'Is it in a bookcase?'

They went wild again.

'Behind a book?'

He didn't respond.

'In a book?' asked Jermaine.

The eyes were now going berserk. How he was going to communicate *A Christmas Carol*, he had no idea until he looked down at his Fitbit.

'So, I just have to guess the name of the book.'

Felix kept looking at the Fitbit.

'Fitbit...Birthday present.'

He rolled his eyes.

'The book's called *Birthday Present*.'

Another blank look.

'I don't know. Or was it a Christmas present as well?'

The eyes rolled.

'*Christmas Present* then.'

Blank.

'Christmas Present...,' shouted Jermaine. 'The ghost of Christmas Present... *A Christmas Carol*!'

Felix's eyes were rolling like they were never going to stop.

Jermaine disappeared after that, and Felix was left alone until Mrs Higgins came in a bit later.

'Now, Felix. I have a special visitor for you, who's going to try and make you better,' she said, giving him a little wink. And in walked Ivy.

'I shall leave you alone with her,' she said, going out and shutting the door behind her.

'So, Felix. You want to get better, and you know that I could get Julius to do that in a second. If you were back in TWAWKI, you could at least be kept alive in hospital. But they can't do that here. No life support or drips or anything like that. You're just going to have to go without nourishment and fade away. The same goes for Edith. You probably don't understand why a Sagacitor would want to do something like this. Well, I'm afraid I must. In order to become queen of this island – like the Queen of England that I once was. That time, I was only queen for nine days before I was executed. This time, I will rule for over fifty years. Fancy trying to undermine my plans. They're great plans and everyone here on Hollow Island will benefit from them, particularly the spirits. What a pity that you wanted to get in the way. Goodbye, Felix.'

And that was it, until Jermaine appeared shortly afterwards.

'You could have kept her talking for a bit longer. Only joking. Right, don't speak. Oh, no. You can't anyway, of course.'

He stood very still.

'Julius, Julius, Julius. Could I have a word with you, please?'

Nothing.

'Julius, Julius, Julius. Give light unto this most sacred of souls.'

The room shook.

'Ah, Julius. Your work has been exemplary.'

Where on earth did he get that word from? Probably the book, thought Felix.

'You have done your worst. And now it is time to do your best. Please remove all the infections that you have planted on this island – forthwith!'

And with that, Felix sat up and walked.

'You legend,' he shouted, unable to believe that he'd recovered so quickly. 'Let's go and get Edith.'

She too was back on her feet in seconds and the three of them sneaked down to Ivy's cottage. Jermaine knocked on the door while Edith and Felix hid round the side.

'Oh, Ivy,' said Jermaine as she answered. 'Someone told me you wanted to see me.'

'Yes, Jermaine. How kind of you to come. Please come in. Take a seat.'

The door was shut but they could still hear what was being said.

'Julius, you have done your best. Now...'

'Hang on,' interrupted Ivy. 'Julius belongs to me...'

'Not anymore. Now, you can do your worst again.'

All they could hear after that was a shriek followed by a thump.

'Good work, Jermaine,' they shouted as they realised that was their cue to go in.

'Seems to have worked. She went out like a light.'

He was wasting no time though.

'And now your best!!!' he said as he stood over Jo, who promptly sat upright on the sofa. 'And now you may go. Thank you, Julius.'

'Yes, thank you, Julius,' said Felix as the front door opened and shut behind them. 'You can return to **your** *House for Lost Souls* now.'

They all stood still for a second until Edith broke the silence.

'Welcome back, Jo. How are you feeling?'

'Oh, good.'

'Do you think that you can do a job for us. We've got a little delivery that needs to be made. What's the old traffic like between here and TWAWKI at the moment?'

'Should be fine. If I go now – before the other collectors start up again. How long have I been out for?'

'Oh, about a day.'

'Should be OK.'

'But if she gets taken home, won't she just start messing up people's lives back on TWAWKI?' said Jermaine.

'Well, good luck to her is all I can say,' answered Edith. 'She's powerless there without the spirits.'

'Well, then, she might try and come back here again,' said Felix. 'If she wakes up before six in the morning, that is.'

'No, she won't. She can't,' said Jo. 'She's tried to be a collector. She's tried alright. She's got me to give her lessons every day. But they never worked. You have to have the right touch; you know what I mean. It's not just about spinning those planium tops. It's the **way** that you spin them. If she wants to come back, she will have to be collected. Don't get me wrong, she'll try everything to come back. She loves it here, but none of the collectors will pick her up now. Not until she's changed her ways, not until she's repented...OK, I'll do it.'

Felix and Edith did a silent hurrah.

'Well, there's no time like...'

'The present!' said Jo, as he pulled out his planium tops and set them spinning on the floor. He picked Ivy up from the chair, held her in his arms and had a look of deep concentration on his face.

'See you in five, guys!'

As soon as he was off, Felix and Edith went up to the attic to see how Mrs Harrington was doing.

'Um. Is that my bobolate?' she said.

'Uh. No. But we can make you some if you like.'

'Have I been asleep?'

'Yes, you must have dropped off for a while. We'll be right back with the bobolate.'

'Thank you, dear. I haven't seen you before, have I? You must be new.'

'Yes, I am.'

They went downstairs and fixed Mrs Harrington's order, which Edith then took up to her.

Minutes later, Jo reappeared in the living room.

'How was that, Jo?' asked Felix.

'Yeah, perfect. She woke up just as I was leaving and got out of bed. So, I know she's recovered. And I made enough noise to wake her parents up, who got up and went to check her room seconds after I was out of sight.'

'Good work, Jo,' said Edith as she reappeared. 'Do you

think that you can take Felix back as well? He needs a fresh start.'

'If you like, although we better get on with it. The second years are coming back tomorrow.'

'Are they?'

'Yes. All the collectors have recovered, of course. Adrian's already back in business. I just met him on the flight path. The rest of them are going to do a full-on day tomorrow. There's a lot of very restless second years, sitting up in bed twiddling their thumbs, waiting to be picked up.'

'Why do people keep coming back?' Felix said to Jo. 'Surely, you'll have done everything you need to after the first year's over.'

'Oh, no. That's just the beginning. As you get older, you're allowed to go to some of the other islands.'

'What happens there?'

'Well, on certain islands, some people actually live out one of their previous lives, twenty-four hours a day.'

'Wow!'

'And properly too. They morph into that person, just like you would have done in the Warriors room, and then they stay as that person. They can then teach you how they used their powers as Sagacitors on TWAWKI. There's one island that's full of musicians. I can't wait to go there. My greatest ambition is to meet Jimi Hendrix.'

'Oh, wow. Is he there? We're going to have to come back. He's my favourite, man.'

'Yeah, you'll come back all right,' said Edith. 'You just need to have a fresh start, Felix, that's all.'

'Yes, I'll come back again next year,' said Felix. 'By then, everyone will know what really happened. What about you, Jermaine?'

'I was just beginning to enjoy it here,' said Jermaine. 'But it wouldn't be the same without my best mate.'

'We better get going for now, though. Our work is done here.'

'OK. When do you want to go?' asked Jo.

'In about half an hour. Just got to say goodbye to Mrs Higgins.'

They walked up the hill to Mrs Higgins' and told her all about everything that had happened to them. She listened intently as they told her what the plan was.

'Would you mind telling the head teacher what has happened, Mrs Higgins?'

'I will. Don't you worry, I'll explain everything. I knew that there was something strange about that girl the moment I set eyes on her.'

'Sorry to say goodbye, Mrs Higgins.'

'So am I. I see people come and go, year in and year out. So, I should be used to this by now. But I'm not. And not with you two. I'm going to admit to having a real soft spot for you boys. Just when I thought we were all nice and settled. You will come back, won't you. I'm going to miss you...'

'Bye, Edith. See you at school, tomorrow,' said Felix. 'Or rather...'

'...In a year's time,' she said.

'Yeah. In a year's time.'

Jo and Felix went out onto the cliff top, from where they

could just see that Stonehenge was back to its normal colour. They then prepared themselves for the journey home. Just as Felix was about to close his eyes though, he was distracted by his friend – the dragonfly – who had landed on his shoulder.

'Oh, you've come to say goodbye. I'll miss you, but I'm coming back.'

It fluttered its wings but made no attempt to move.

'You can't come with me. I'm going back to TWAWKI,' Felix explained.

'Who you talking to, man?' said Jo, as he set the tops in motion.

'I was just saying to my friend – the dragonfly – that he can't come with me. But he won't budge.'

'Don't worry about insects, man.'

'I think he might be a bit more than that.'

'Doesn't matter,' said Jo, gathering up the tops. 'It's you that's important. Right, off we go!'

As with the last time, Felix felt himself being pulled in both directions until, that is, he passed out. The next thing he knew was that he was back in his bedroom at Trevelyan Tower, very quietly saying his goodbyes to Jo. After he'd gone, he looked at his Fitbit. Quarter past twelve. That was all right. He shouldn't be too sleepy the next day at school after all. What about the dragonfly though? He put his hand into his jacket pocket and fished out what felt like a piece of jewellery. His insect friend had turned to stone, even though its multi-coloured scales were glittering as much as they ever had done. He held him in his hand and just looked at him.

But then, there it was again. That presence that he'd felt in his room just before he'd set off for Hollow Island.

He wrapped the dragonfly up in tissue paper and hid it away in a drawer and got ready for bed. As he was putting on his pyjamas though, he heard a noise outside the door and poked his head round to see what it was. His dad was sitting on the sofa with his head in his hands.

'Dad,' said Felix, giving him a bit of a nudge.

'Yes,' muttered his dad. 'Sorry, Son. Did I wake you?'

'No, I was still up.' If only he knew!

'I didn't want to disturb you.'

'Well, you didn't.'

'It's your grandpa.'

'What do you mean?'

'He pressed his alarm button, and I went down to see him. I was hoping you wouldn't hear.'

'Oh, yes. I did hear you go out,' he said, remembering.

'Well, it happened shortly after that. Just as I went into the flat.'

'What happened?'

'He was very peaceful, Son. I would have come and told you, but I didn't want to wake you.'

'Do you mean he's...'

'Yes, Son.'

'Oh, no. Oh, I knew this was going to happen.'

'Yes, so did he.'

They both stood looking at the floor for some considerable time until Felix broke the silence.

'What time did he die?'

'I did look at my watch as it happens. Sometimes people ask you these things. 23.45.'

'Oh.'

'About 25 minutes ago. I left the ambulance crew to sort everything out.'

'Did Grandpa like dragonflies?' said Felix after a while.

'What are you on about, Son?'

'Oh, nothing.'

'I think he did, now you mention it. Anyways, you get yourself to bed.'

'I will.'

'What's happened to your hand, Son?'

'Got bitten by a dog.'

'Oh, I didn't notice that before. You kept that hidden.'

'It's alright. It's all been disinfected properly.'

'Where is this dog now? Do you know who's it was?'

'Yes. It's been dealt with, Dad. I think it's learnt its lesson.'

'Oh, alright, Son. Goodnight.'

'Goodnight, Dad.'

'Goodnight, Son. We'll get through this.'

'Yeah, Dad. We will.'

END OF BOOK 1

BE THE FIRST TO READ THE OPENING CHAPTER OF:

Felix Featherstone and The Tunnel of Treasures (Part 2 of The Hollow Island Trilogy)

On November 29th the following year, Felix woke up with a start to the sound of chattering outside his window. Considering he lived on the sixth floor of a tower block, this was not a common occurrence. In fact, it had only happened once before. The time they sent the window cleaners to abseil down the building and clear off all the grime and bird poo that had accumulated over the years.

But it was not the window cleaners who were outside this time, and he was not in his bedroom either. And quite apart from all that, it was 10.30 at night. As he came to, he realised that he was lying on a sofa in the maintenance shed in The Under – the safe-haven that Edith had arranged for him. She had sent him a key to ensure that he was well away from any of the collectors on the nights leading up to Holloween. Why? Felix had no idea as Edith had moved up north and kept her communication to a minimum. All he did know was that his life was in mortal danger if he went to Hollow Island that year.

'I think that Kevin said that it was the key with the yellow cover on it,' said one of the people outside. 'Yes, and he said he left his passport in the top drawer of the desk,' said the other. This was Felix's cue to get out of there and as soon as he heard a key being inserted into the lock, he picked up all his belongings, sneaked into the shower room, opened its window, and climbed out of the back of the shed. As he put his shoes and jumper on behind one of the pillars, he watched as a man and a woman, wearing the same logoed t-shirts, opened the door and went in. Edith had assured him that the shed was only used on Tuesdays and Fridays but that obviously didn't take into account occasional visits from other parties – such as this one.

'Unlike Kevin to leave the shower room window open,' said the woman. 'He's usually very security conscious.' But Felix didn't wait around to hear the response. He was off.

He had to go somewhere that a collector wouldn't find him. Although Edith hadn't come back to school that Autumn term, he'd had texts on a daily basis from her, telling him not to go to the party this year. Whenever he texted her back and said, 'Do you mean the HOLLOW... party?', she said 'Yes. Under no circumstances should you go!!' He would then respond with something like: 'Why? Am I still Public Enemy Number 1?' and she would say 'No, far from it.' But she still wouldn't explain why he shouldn't go. All she would do was to keep sending him messages every day, saying 'DO NOT GO TO THE PARTY.' That was strange enough. But then the world was in a bit of a strange place as it was. Oil refineries all over Europe and America had become solidified, which meant that products like petrol had had to be heavily rationed. Also, the fuel tanks of almost all the private jets and helicopters around the world had frozen up. Even scientists couldn't explain how this could have happened.

As Felix made his way out of The Under, he noticed that Jermaine's light was on in his bedroom – which was on the ground floor. So, he gave it a knock.

'What's going down, Flix?' he said, sticking his head out.

'Someone else is using my hideout.'

'Oh, right.'

'Can I stay here tonight?'

'Yeah. Should be alright. But my mum's ill and Dad's asleep in the living room. So, you're going to just not use the bathroom – unless you want to make my dad think he's seen a ghost in the middle of the night. Climb in, mate.'

'Oh, thanks. I won't stay long. I'll head off somewhere else in the morning. Would you mind telling Miss that I'm not coming in for a few days.'

'Yeah, sure.'

'She'll want to see a note. But I don't want her calling my dad. I told him I was coming here for a couple of days, and he'll be thinking I'm still going to school.'

'Well, why don't you?' he said.

'Because...I need to get as far away from any of the collectors as is humanly possible. Are you still going?'

'Too right. That's why I need some beauty sleep. Sofa's all yours, mate.'

'Great. Thanks, Jermaine. You're the best.'

'Goodnight.'

And within minutes, the sounds of the traffic and the foxes outside were drowned out by the gentle and the not-so-gentle snores that were competing with each other inside the room.

In the middle of the night however, Felix was woken up by something blowing in through the window, which Jermaine had left ajar. It was like a handful of dust, and it missed Felix but went all over Jermaine's bed. For a moment, he thought that he should wake him up, but then again, his beauty sleep was not to be disturbed.

The next morning, before it was even light, Felix got up as quietly as he could and started to climb back out of the window.

'I'll see you when you get back,' he said, but there was no answer. In fact, there wasn't a sound or even a snore coming from him. Felix thought maybe this time he should wake him up to let him know about the dust. So, he got down from the window ledge and put his hand on Jermaine's shoulder. No response. He grabbed hold of his arm and gave it a bit of a shaking. Nothing. It seemed like he was unconscious.

Felix opened the bedroom door just as Mr Toussaint was getting up from the sofa.

'Oh, hi, Mr T. I just stayed the...'

'I know. I heard you.'

'Oh, right.'

'No problem, Felix. You can come and stay whenever you want.'

'Thank you...Um, I'm a bit worried about Jermaine. He doesn't seem to want to wake up.'

'That's his biggest problem in life. He'd never get out of bed if he had his own way.'

'No, but he seems to be unconscious.'

'Really. Let me have a look.'

So, they went back into the bedroom and Mr T gave him another shake. Nothing.

'This usually does the trick,' said Mr T as he pinched him on the side and tickled his rib cage. Nothing.

'He's got some dreaded lurgy. No two ways about it. You better get off. Don't want you getting it too.'

'No, I suppose not. I wish I could do something to help.'

'Getting out of here will be a start. Oh, Lord. This is bad, very bad.'

So, Felix grabbed his things and went out of the door.

'Goodbye, Mr T. I'll give you a ring later and see how he's doing.'

'You do that. Goodbye, Felix.'

The streets were empty apart from the foxes, who stared at him blankly as though he wasn't there. It almost made him wish that he could see the wolveraffes again. At least he had had some kind of relationship with those long-necked wolf-like creatures, even if they had behaved like guardians one moment and savages the next.

He had no idea where he was going. He was just going. So, he went into the tube station at Latimer Road and got on the first train that stopped there.

Just as he was wondering what to do next, an announcement was made on the tube to say that the train was terminating at Liverpool Street. Following all the other passengers, he got out there, went up the escalator and walked through the ticket barrier onto the railway station concourse. Hordes of passengers were pouring out of the numerous platforms. Ever since the oil crisis, unless you had an electric car, you had to travel by rail. But these were all people coming into London, not going out and they were heading for the tube. There was no point in him going back down there. He'd just get caught in the crush. Someone pushed past him and said, 'Platform 10, son. That's what you're after.' So, without even thinking, Felix walked in that direction. As they'd left all the barrier gates open, he squeezed through the crowd coming out of that platform and got on the nearest train – which pulled out of the station shortly afterwards.

As they zipped through the English countryside, Felix sat wondering where he was going to end up. And then after about an hour of his journey, the automatic doors opened, and a big, tall, chestnut-coloured dog came marching down the aisle. It was almost as if it knew Felix and had been looking for him. It came straight over, greeted him with a lick and settled down next to him as if he was its owner.

Shortly afterwards, the guard came through.

'Tickets from Liverpool Street,' she said.

'Oh, I need to get a ticket to...'

'Ipswich?'

'Yes,' he said even though he had no idea where he was going.

'That'll be £28.85.'

'Oh, I don't think I've got that much.'

'Name? Address?'

He gave her all his details and she asked him why he wasn't at school. So, he said something about trouble at home and asked her if she knew anything about the dog that was now lying across his feet. A quick glance down at the floor was followed by a suspicious look into his eyes.

'Which dog?'

'This one. It's not mine,' he answered.

'Well, in that case, I suggest that the first thing you do when you get to Ipswich is to go straight to the police station. You can tell them about your dog and, while you're about it, you can tell them everything that you've just told me.'

'Oh, alright. Thank you, miss.'

When the train pulled up at Ipswich Station, the dog immediately got up and headed for the exit. As soon as the doors opened, he bounded out, lingered for a moment on the platform and then lead the way, looking round all the time to check that Felix was following. As they walked up the road towards the town, he spotted the Police Station and stopped still outside it. His German Pointer friend was already a hundred yards ahead of him though and simply stood there expectantly, waiting for him to join him.

'No, come back here!' Felix called out. But he didn't. He just stayed where he was. When Felix went to get him, he started off again. So, he grabbed his collar and tried to pull him back, but he wouldn't budge. So, Felix let go and the dog continued walking – seeming to know exactly where he was going.

Eventually, they came to a lane with an old farmhouse at the end of it. His friend immediately turned into it, led him to the front door and started to bark. This set off a whole cacophony of howls and growls from the other side, until the door was opened, and it all died down. Tails were wagging right, left and centre and an assortment of dogs were jumping up and licking his hands.

'Well, someone's popular,' said a voice from behind the door and a woman, wearing a sloppy jumper and jeans, appeared.

'Um. I found this dog on a train from London, and he's just brought me here.'

'Oh. Probably because this is where the party is – for dogs anyway. He's obviously heard about it through the Ipswich grapevine...Where have you come from?'

'London.'

'And where are you going now?'

'I don't know,' said Felix. 'Probably back to London.'

'So why did you come all the way up here?'

He could have just said 'trouble at home', like he did to the ticket inspector, but then he thought of something which was true, even if it had happened a year ago.

'I've sort of run away. My dad's girlfriend said something

that hurt me and I'm afraid I threw a bowl of washing up water all over her.'

'Does that mean you need somewhere to stay?'

'Maybe. I'm not sure.'

'Well, you might as well come in and have a cup of tea while you're thinking about it. My pack of hounds have obviously taken to you. So, you can always stay with them in The Kennel. And your new friend can join you... Where is this dog, by the way?'

But just at that moment, Felix's new friend ran off down the lane. As he didn't know his name, he couldn't call him back.

'He's there,' he said, pointing down the lane.

'Is he? Oh, yes...Don't worry. He knows what he's doing. If he can commute to London and back, he should be able to look after himself. Anyway, come in,' she said as she closed the door. 'Cup of tea?'

'Thank you,' said Felix as they went into the farmhouse kitchen with a roaring fire crackling away at the other end. He went and stood by it to warm himself up and looked at all the photographs on the mantlepiece. There was one that he couldn't take his eyes off.

'Is that your, son?' he said, pointing to a photograph of a boy with long, black hair.

'Yes, Joseph. He'll be back in a minute. He's got a couple of days off school because of the oil crisis.'

'Oh, blimey! I know him,' said Felix. It was Jo, the collector who'd lived in Ivy's cottage last year.

'Do you?' said the woman.

'Yes,' he said.

'Where do you know him from? He's never been to London.'

'Oh, no. I met him...somewhere else...at a party.'

'Oh, I see...What, up here?'

'Yes,' he said. 'A sort of...um... Halloween party.'

'Oh, yes. He likes those.'

It was at that moment that the front door opened and then slammed shut again almost immediately afterwards.

'Joseph!'

'Yeah, Mum.'

'Come into the kitchen. There's someone here to see you.'

'Oh. OK...'

And in came Joseph, with his trade-mark locks, looking almost the same as Felix had last seen him when he'd delivered him back to his flat from Hollow Island last year.

'Felix!'

'Felix might be staying with us for a couple of nights...'

'...If that's OK.'

'Of course it's OK. I've just offered, haven't I. You'll be happy with that, won't you, Jo?'

'Yeah, of course. He's got to stay. Now that he's come all the way up here from...London, isn't it?'

'Yes.'

'I gather that you met Felix at a party.'

'Oh, yeah. That's right. We met at a party, didn't we!'

'Perhaps you could show him The Kennel.'

'Oh, yeah. This way, man.'

They went out of the back of the kitchen through some French Windows and towards a converted barn.

'Oh. Wow!' said Felix as they walked into a room with sofas, rugs, a large TV and a sound system.

'Welcome to The Kennel. Your bedroom's in there and mine's upstairs.'

'I could stay here for weeks.'

'Steady. We'll be off tonight.'

'Oh, no. I'm not going this year.'

'You're not going?'

But Jo's mum put her head round the door at that moment, clutching a whole lot of leads.

The dogs looked up expectantly.

'Joseph, do you think you could...'

'Oh, yeah. No worries. Are you coming, Felix?'

'What, for a walk?'

That was the word that the dogs had been waiting for. There was barking, there was howling, there was jumping up with joy and the little Jack Russell was so over-excited that it couldn't keep still for Felix to put the lead on. They took three each and then set off down the lane, letting them loose as they went through a gate.

As they walked, Felix explained to Joseph about Edith's texts, warning him not to come. He also told him how frustrated he had been at home all year.

Meanwhile, the dogs tore through the fields, disappearing into the morning mist – which floated just above the ground – and then reappearing a few minutes later. They ran back towards them with renewed vigour, as if they'd just returned from some far-off world.

'Felix, there is one thing that stands out a mile from everything that you've just said,' said Jo. 'You need to get away, man. To have some space from the claustrophobia of your dad's flat. I know it's only for a few hours in our time. But it won't feel like it because it'll be a year in Tritan time.'

'Yeah, you're right. Life back here on Earth feels so meaningless after what I went through on Hollow Island last year. I was a man of action when I was there. Here, I'm nothing.'

'Too right,' said Jo.

'And I love that island. All the cliffs and coves, Mrs Higgins' cottage with its beautiful views out to sea. She's not going be happy if both Jermaine and I don't turn up.'

'What do you mean?'

'Jermaine's gone down with something really weird.'

'Oh. I'm supposed to be picking him up later. I'll go and check up on him.'

'You do that,' said Felix.

'In the meantime, you should definitely go to Hollow Island. I can't see what the danger is.'

'Well, you yourself said that there was a lot of evil on the island amongst some of the guides.'

'I know. But that was when I was under the influence, so to speak – when I was being hypnotised by Ivy. I wasn't thinking straight. I don't feel that anymore. In fact, the only person who could cause you any harm would be Ivy. And there's no way that she can get back there on her own.'

'How come? If she was able to tap into all those magical powers...'

'Because she'd have to be a collector.'

'Oh, yes. You told me. She couldn't get the hang of spinning the planium tops properly.'

'So, there's nothing to be afraid of. You sorted everything out last year. You're an absolute hero because of that. In fact, I can't think of any reason why you shouldn't go this year. Everyone will be looking after you and keeping an eye out for you.'

'Yeah, I suppose so. So, they've forgiven me for all my outbursts.'

'Yeah, man. They know exactly where all that came from. And the only reason you can't find out what Edith means in her texts is because she can't spell it out in black and white. She has to write in code and talk like we did with my mum – about parties. The only way you can find out properly is if you go to Hollow Island and ask her. If there really is a reason, I'll bring you back again.'

'But that wouldn't be for a couple of weeks. Remember what happened with Jermaine.'

'I do. But that was because you arrived right at the beginning. This year, you'd be going in the last batch. About ten days later. Or rather ten minutes later, our time. Are you in or are you out?'

'I'm in.'

Milton Keynes UK
Ingram Content Group UK Ltd.
UKHW040706260324
440035UK00001B/1